Born to Lose
Tales of Gigi
Marek Z. Turner

Poliziotturner

Poliziotturner Press

BORN TO LOSE: TALES OF GIGI

Copyright © 2025 Marek Z. Turner

All rights reserved. No part of this book may be reproduced or transmitted in any form or by any electronic or mechanical means, including photocopying, recording or by any information and retrieval system, without the written permission of the publisher and author, except where permitted by law. No part of this book may be used or reproduced in any manner for the purpose of training artificial intelligence technologies or systems. In accordance with Article 4(3) of the Digital Single Market Directive 2019/790 Marek Z. Turner expressly reserves this work from the text and data mining exception.

This novel is a work of fiction. The author reserves all rights to be recognised as the owner of this work.

Cover artwork by Marco Marella.

ISBN: 978-1-7392916-3-1 (Print)

ISBN: 978-1-7392916-2-4 (Digital)

First printing 2025.

Contents

Acknowledgements	IV
1. A Cop's Sting	1
2. Low Hanging Fruit	14
3. Running on Fumes	17
4. 137 Words to Salvation	22
5. A Real Pizza Work	25
6. The Card Sharps	31
7. In a Real State	35
8. To Kill a Prosecutor	40
9. Dance of Suspicion	86
10. Luck Be a Lady	90
11. Stolen Time	110
12. About the author	141

Acknowledgements

Gigi? Wait, isn't he that guy from...? Yeah, that's right.

This collection started with being bored and stuck in traffic during my daily commute. Sat there in a static vehicle, I had nothing to do but think back on the recently watched Dario Argento giallo '*Cat O' Nine Tails*', and somehow my predicament of being in a car going nowhere meshed with that of the films unlucky crook, Gigi (wonderfully played by Ugo Fangareggi) and by the time I arrived at work an hour later, the story '*Running on Fumes*' was born.

I initially intended this story to be a bit of fun, which I could share online and use to hone my craft. Then I wrote another short, the sillier '*A Real Pizza Work*', and found that I was having so much fun exploring this character that I didn't want to stop and before I knew it, this collection was born.

However, on more than a handful of occasions, I wondered if what I was doing was right. After all, the wonderful trio of Dario Argento, Luigi Cozzi and Dardano Sacchetti created the initial premise of the perennially unlucky thief Gigi, and while my character differed notably (I even considered changing the name but it didn't suit him) his inspiration certainly fell into what I felt was a grey area.

Eventually, having finished the stories for this collection, I threw caution to the wind and embraced it. This resulted in two flash pieces that tie in with the movie.

So, I hope Dario, Luigi, and Dardano take this collection in the spirit in which it is meant.

I would also like to thank Giles David Edwards and Tom Woods for their help with developing my writing in their own unique ways, and for Dea Parkin and Fiction Feedback who have helped show me the error of my ways on several occasions.

Finally, I dedicate this collection to Sienna and Lara.

A Cop's Sting

The hard wooden chair reminded Gigi of the type used for interrogations in local police stations. No matter how he shifted his body, he couldn't get comfortable. With a final twist of his torso, his coat slid off the chair and landed on the grimy floor. He moved to pick it up, but the table poked into his ribs and caused him to reconsider. He sighed his acceptance and looked around the rundown, single-storey bar. Although he'd visited the impoverished area of Falchera before, it was his first time in this particular dump, and he hoped it would be his last.

Shaking his head, he picked up his drink and stared at its discoloured rim, the finger marks on the outside, and the bubbles that stuck to the inside. He shrugged and forced down some of the tepid beer before returning the glass to its place on a stained chequered tablecloth.

After using the back of his hand to wipe his mouth dry, he shifted his attention to the old man who was propping up the bar. Michelangelo Moggi. His mentor.

Gigi watched as Moggi leaned forward, his forearms resting on the counter, and stared at a single shot of whisky in front of him.

The two of them had only been working together for a few years, but during that time Gigi had come a long way. A long way from innocence, for sure. Moggi opened up an unconventional world of opportunity for Gigi and his locksmithing skills, as well as the nous on how to operate in this new environment.

As a team, they'd won several large contracts while sticking to their principles. This approach made them a tidy sum, and, perhaps even better for Gigi, a reputation he could finally be proud of.

Gigi never saw much of the money, though, preferring to trust it to the prudent investments managed by his mentor. Or at least he thought so. Turns out those financial ventures had been in green-felt-and-card stock.

Then the day came when four heavies set them up and beat them down. Moggi admitted the level of his gambling debts and that their partnership's account was wiped out.

Left penniless, they had no choice but to take any work that came their way. And that was when a man known only as Truffa contacted Moggi. He claimed to represent a foreign corporation and offered him a handsome payment to steal some documents from an office in the Lingotto Fiat factory. The old man agreed in a heartbeat.

Four days after the commission, the production line, coerced by the left-wing group Lotta Continua, downed tools and waged a two-day protest against the owners. Gigi knew there'd be no better opportunity, and the duo went to work. They snuck in while wearing high-visibility jackets, muttered some words about workers' rights and found themselves in the chief engineer's office. Once inside, taking the documents from a cheap filing cabinet was child's play. They even had time to use the office phone to call Truffa, who promptly instructed them to come to this bar for the exchange.

Ever cautious, Gigi had 'borrowed' a car from a dealership on the other side of the city, planning to return it before the place opened in the morning. They parked a short walk away, tucked down a side alley. The location meant that even if someone reported the vehicle as missing, their means of escape was unlikely to be seen, at least not until it was too late.

Lost in thought about what led them here, a hacking cough returned Gigi's mind to the bar. He took a swig of his drink, checked out a couple of women sitting a few tables to his right and finally looked over at his friend, who'd leaned back, fist in mouth, stifling his continuous barking.

Moggi spluttered for another minute, and his oval face soon resembled a *dattarini* tomato. After recovering, he raised a liver-spotted hand and ordered a second whisky.

Gigi sucked in some stale air and glanced at his watch. The client was late.

At that moment the front door screeched open and a short, thin man in a black fitted three-piece suit strolled in. He had a pencil moustache, groomed hair and looked out of place in the almost decrepit surroundings of split wooden beams and cracked plastic tables.

Following him was a heavy-set guy who, dressed in faded jeans and a brown jacket over a blue shirt, could have passed for a regular. The man was a bruiser, no doubt about it. As he walked, his thick neck swept right to left, while his right hand remained attached to an object poking out of his trouser waistband. A clear signal to everyone he was carrying and ready for action.

As the men approached Moggi, Gigi's heart pounded, and his eyes flitted between the client and his gorilla.

Moggi stood and greeted the diminutive man with a light kiss on both cheeks, but before the men could take their seats, the gorilla shouted toward the barista, complaining about the perceived slow service.

After giving their order, Moggi and Truffa sat down facing each other, and talked. The bruiser remained standing but had positioned his body to survey the other patrons. His hard stare soon rested on Gigi.

Whether it was the stale beer, or the overwhelming disdain painted on the gorilla's face, the contents of Gigi's stomach swirled around, and a bitter tang settled at the back of his throat. He glanced away, feigning interest in the flaking yellow paint on a nearby wall.

Recognising the gravelly chuckle, Gigi looked back at the group and saw that not only had the thug turned away, but that now Moggi was looking at him.

The old man nodded at his protégé. The deal was on.

Gigi slowly rose, and as he pushed the table to the side, hiding his coat from view, its legs scraped against the floor and made him wince.

He made his way to retrieve the documents from the bathroom – arriving early to stash the goods at the handover point was another safety precaution the duo used, to ensure they were never nabbed with evidence on them – Gigi stole a glance at the client, and for the first time noticed his scuffed brown shoes, resting on the lower rung of the bar stool. He didn't know why, but something seemed off.

While he walked down the narrow corridor that led to the toilets, he pondered on why a well-dressed man would have dirty shoes. As he entered the area that passed for a bathroom: one urinal, one cubicle, a sink, and a large mirror. He looked at himself and shrugged. *Who knows what those rich bastards did? Dirty shoes. Dirty hands.* He chuckled at the thought as he knew his job now would see his own hands get filthy, although in a much more literal way.

Ever practical, Moggi had sealed the stolen documents in a waterproof ziplock bag and placed it in the cistern of the only toilet in the bathroom. Another neat little trick that proved the old guy still had it where it counted. So, if things turned to polenta, then the goods were secure and could be retrieved at a later date.

Because his task was so simple, Gigi knew he had time to make himself look a little more presentable before returning to the bar. He could use his meagre cut to treat the ladies. With cheap alcohol and even cheaper women on his mind, Gigi walked across to the sink and ran the tap. He turned his face from side to side and patted water on his cheeks.

He was halfway through restyling his messy hair when another man walked in, blowing great gusts of air out of his ruddy cheeks and from elsewhere too, judging by the odour that followed him.

Gigi watched in horror as the bumbling man staggered towards the only cubicle. Before Gigi could open his mouth to protest, the man's wide body lunged forward. He threw out one hand at the door frame, but his momentum was too much and the wooden door gave way, sending the man spinning around and crashing back to the floor with a bang.

Gigi rushed to help the man who was sitting on his arse next to the stained porcelain toilet.

He placed his hands under the man's elbows and lifted him up. The pungent stench of meat, cabbage and beer erupted from the man's mouth with a loud burp before he pushed Gigi back out of the stall, called him a pervert and slammed the door in his face. The hinges rattled and the rickety wooden frame of the cubicle shook.

Then came the worst sound he could imagine as the man settled in for what Gigi suspected might be a long shift.

Gigi paced between the cubicle and the main door, running his fingers through his semi-styled hair and wondering what to do.

He needed to get in there and grab those documents. As he turned for the fifth lap, he noticed the pipes that ran along the foot of the back wall and into the cubicle.

His eyes sparkled under the dim glow of the overhead strip light.

He dashed over and, assessing the assortment of uncovered valves and taps, rotated them at random. Soon enough, a hissing sound like a snake emanated from the cubicle and was followed by a loud bang from the direction of the sinks. The intensity of the water hammer increased, its deep knocking sound filling the room while the pipes rattled with the ferocity of an innocent man imprisoned.

Gigi took a step back towards the main door as the man in the cubicle started shouting. Although his words were slurred, the meaning was clear. Help.

A loud pop caused Gigi to duck down. It was followed by an ominous silence that seemed to suffocate the room.

'Hello?' said the man on the toilet, breaking the tension, just before an explosion of water sent him flying out of the cubicle and into the front panel of the sink unit with a dull thud.

Gigi stared at the man, his trousers and underwear down by his ankles. Murky water sloshed around the contours of his semi-naked body.

The creaking cubicle door swung back into place with a snap.

There was no time to lose. Gigi stepped around the man, opened the cubicle door, and crept inside. Meanwhile the man, oblivious, clambered to his feet, pulled up his wet clothing and muttered obscenities as he waddled out of the bathroom.

Now standing in the the enclosed space, Gigi rolled his tongue over his top front teeth, and moved toward the cistern. At the smell of the brown water his lips curled up and his nose wrinkled. It was worse than when he'd found himself in solitary confinement a few years ago. Still, he continued, and with each step the water soaked the bottom of his jeans a little more, seeped into his socks and filled every available space in his shoes.

A loud but muffled voice caused him to pause. 'Go on, look at it. I could have been killed,' said the man. 'Look.'

Gigi shoved the ajar door closed. It creaked back open so he put his shoulder into it, forcing it shut, before bolting the lock. The last thing he wanted was for someone to come in and ask him questions. What good ever came from being asked a question?

He shook his head and told himself to concentrate on the job. Then he set about lifting the cistern lid. The porcelain top came off with little effort, and he placed it across the now lowered toilet seat.

He peered in and from the near-empty cistern withdrew a folded-over A4 plastic wallet. He shook it out, sending droplets of stale water all over his trousers, before unzipping it, dropping the wallet to the floor and shoving the dry documents under his jumper and into his waistband.

Satisfied the deal could now proceed, he turned and pulled on the door.

No movement.

He tried again with more force.

The door didn't budge.

He bit his lip and appraised the situation. If he failed to return soon, Moggi was likely for it. The type of people who ordered industrial espionage weren't known for their patience. Not to mention, the longer Gigi took, the more likely it was that the owners would come in to deal with this watery mess. That meant more people taking note of who was here, and more people to point the finger if things went wrong.

Being inconspicuous was easy when nothing happened, but being stuck in a flooded bathroom didn't exactly qualify as an uneventful situation.

Gigi exhaled, tensed his shoulders and chest, and with the space afforded to him, which barely amounted to two steps, he charged the cubicle door, his lead foot slipping in the watery sludge.

A small yelp escaped his mouth as the door rattled – and so did his bones as he slid down into the fetid water.

Hauling himself to his feet, he shook out his arms, spraying liquid all around, before noticing that a thread of his woollen jumper had snagged on a hinge. He swore under his breath.

It was a new sweater as well. Expensive. Paid for from the proceeds of his last job. A rare success that had filled him with such confidence, he went out and updated his winter wardrobe. After all, it got cold in Torino during these months, but someone in his line of work couldn't afford to be encumbered by too many layers of clothing, so lightweight quality was key.

He narrowed his eyes and studied the jammed door. Its rusted hinges and stuck bolt had all conspired to keep him prisoner. His nose meanwhile continued to twitch as the foul odour of wastewater filled the room. If nothing else, he had to get out of here for his sanity. He turned on the spot, clicking his thumb and middle finger, the snapping motion allowing him to think through the situation.

He could call for help. It would be embarrassing, but he could live with that for his share of this deal. His mouth opened – but shut before any noise could emerge. If people found out a professional burglar couldn't even escape from a toilet cubicle, it would be the end of his career.

Then an idea hit him. Like a ray of moonlight through the rectangular window above. He was saved. As long as he could fit through.

His right shoe squelched as it pressed on the toilet lid, while his left wobbled on the uneven cistern cover as he pushed himself up and away from the turgid pool of contaminated water that surrounded him.

Gigi unhooked the rusty window latch, then pushed up the frame and poked his head through. As his hands let go of the window, in an attempt to pull himself forward, the frame slowly scraped its way down along the back of his head until it settled onto his neck. In discomfort but satisfied that the coast was clear, he grunted as he hauled his body up.

It took just over a minute to squeeze the top of his shoulders through, and then a further three minutes of wiggling, grimacing, and grunting before finding himself dangling half in and half out, resembling a human seesaw.

By now, the stiff wind had slapped his face raw, and he puffed out misty clouds of cold desperation. He kept on wriggling like a worm on a hook and squirmed past the tipping point, on which he hurtled down into the wet prickly bush beneath.

Thin branches raked at his skin as he sank into the balding greenery. Eventually he rolled off the bush and on to the pavement that ran around the side of the bar.

He stood up and, after checking himself over, ran his palms down his tattered jumper. He continued to brush the remnants of twig, leaf, and grunge off his clothing before realising something was wrong. His hands slapped against his stomach, and the rustle of paper coming from beneath his clothing didn't reassure him. A cold sensation ran over his body as he lifted his clothing, only to see several tears in the document he was supposed to deliver.

People had been killed for less. What if Truffa had connections to the mafia? No, that was ridiculous, wasn't it? As a wave of negativity flooded Gigi's mind, he breathed faster, and the bitter taste of bile pervaded his mouth.

In a state of panic, Gigi laid the documents on the flattest part of the nearby bush and smoothed out the paper. His slow steady palm worked its way from the bottom to the top.

Satisfied that the sheaf of documents was as presentable as it was going to get – the minor tears, while visible, surely wouldn't stop any sale – Gigi picked the pile up and felt the damp bottom. The moisture from a late afternoon downpour now absorbed into the lower pages.

His body temperature rocketed as he turned the sheets of paper over to see more lacerations and smudges. He grabbed several sheets from the middle and shoved them underneath, hoping that would work. At least long enough for he and Moggi to get away.

After clearing his throat and adjusting the sheets of paper one more time, Gigi straightened up and headed down the pathway towards the bar.

Sure, it would seem odd for him to walk in through the front, and he didn't really know what he'd say if they asked why. Perhaps they wouldn't even notice.

As he made it to the corner, a Guardia Di Finanza van screeched to a halt in the parking area directly outside, while a Fiat 128 swerved and skidded to a stop next to it. Armed officers burst out of both vehicles and into the bar.

Gigi slunk back and crouched down behind his bush.

After listening to a few minutes of shouting, he edged forward and watched as the *Guardia* forcibly removed the patrons and made them stand facing the front wall of the bar. Gigi shuffled some more and spotted the soaked waddler, who was protesting the loudest, demanding to be given special treatment after the night he'd endured. He received a face full of crumbling brick for his troubles.

The impromptu line-up seemed a little short, though, and it didn't take Gigi long to realise it was missing Moggi, Truffa, and the brute.

His intuition had been right. Something was up.

With great bluster, the diminutive, well-dressed man burst out through the door and stormed up to a young guy in a creased brown suit. Meanwhile, the gorilla forced Moggi up against the wall.

Gigi's eyes welled up as he witnessed Moggi's knees give way under the force that propelled him forward. His aging body was no match for the gorilla's ferocious shove.

'Where the hell is he?' said the irate posh man to his younger subordinate. 'You burst in too soon, you idiot. I hadn't received the documents!'

The scolding travelled on the wind before descending into a blasphemous diatribe that would have given a priest a coronary.

Gigi wiped his eyes and focused on the angry man, Truffa, who was clearly a captain or lieutenant in the organisation. He watched as the cop stormed over to Moggi, where he ordered his oversized lackey to shove Gigi's associate into the waiting 128. Then they both headed inside; Gigi assumed to search the place.

He shoved the documents back into his waistband and waited until all the remaining officers and patrons were bundled into the van.

Unsure of how long he had before Truffa and his colleague came out again, his feet danced across the grey concrete, and he soon stared into the dimmed eyes of the closest thing he ever had to a father. Cowed and ashen-faced, Moggi cut a sorry figure in the rear of the Fiat. The image made Gigi's heart sink and his gut ache. It was no way to go for a man who had saved Gigi from a life of destitution.

Moggi lifted his head and looked at his protégé. There were no tears in the old man's eyes, only a weariness, or perhaps an acceptance that this was the end.

Gigi turned his gaze toward the door handle and knew that even if it was locked, he could figure out how to get Moggi out. He had to. But then a movement from inside stopped him dead in his tracks.

Moggi shook his head.

Then, with a firm nod, he directed Gigi back into the alleyway.

Gigi hesitated, then his hand reached for the handle. He had to try. Locked. As he looked up to reassure his friend, Moggi suddenly appeared different to him. Smaller. His trials and tribulations were etched on his face. It was only then that Gigi accepted the pleading in his eyes.

He turned his head away, balled up his fists, and began to walk. An impotent anger burned inside. Consumed by frustration, fear, and sorrow, in a haze he walked the few hundred yards across grey concrete and beside graffiti-strewn walls to the backstreet of Via degli Abeti. There he plodded in the darkness to the hot Fiat 500 that had brought them there.

For a couple of minutes, he sat in the passenger seat, resting his head against the top of the steering wheel. The documents dug into his stomach, but he ignored the discomfort and wept for what would happen to Moggi.

Despite his age, despite his ill health, the old man was going to have one last holiday at the state's expense. A final trip.

It took a few minutes before Gigi composed himself, cleared his throat and started the car. In silence, he headed back to the dealership, where he parked up and walked for five minutes to his regular bar, Il Perdente.

Inside, he greeted his fellow regulars with a solemn nod and ordered a J&B whisky. Neat.

'No Angelo tonight?' asked Enrico as he placed the drink on the counter.

Gigi took the glass and stared at it as he swirled the fiery amber liquid. 'No. He won't be in again,' he said before downing the drink and ordering another.

At the end of the evening. and despite his inebriated state, a clarity or rather an acceptance came over his mind. It was time for him to become his own boss.

Low Hanging Fruit

Gigi slanted his body inward and flicked the crumbs off his rumpled black t-shirt and creased army fatigue jacket. He knew he stood out like a rotten tooth in Alberto Sordi's mouth. But what could he do? The suit-wearing client called the meeting at the last minute and chose the location. In all truth, though, even if he had more time, he owned nothing that would have ingratiated him to the group that now sat in the historic Caffè d'oro.

Apparently, the likes of Picasso, Dumas, Puccini, and Hemingway had all drank there, but when Gigi was told this, as he sipped his espresso, he just shrugged. The only artists he cared about represented the Grande Torino football club back in the forties.

But with business now concluded, Gigi sat alone and lost in thought. The job had seemed a simple one, perhaps even a little exciting. Industrial espionage was a growing market, and wrapped up in how he made the most of this lucrative opportunity, he didn't notice the dark cloud descending over him.

The waiter gave a gentle cough.

Gigi glanced up into the wall-mounted mirror in front of him and saw a stern face reflected back.

'Now that your friend has gone, sir, will you be vacating the table?'

He sighed and turned sideways on the slim wooden chair. As he moved, his eyes passed over a half-eaten croissant. Looking up at the waiter, he opened his mouth, but paused. Why? He couldn't say. Perhaps just a heightened sense of his surroundings. The type honed by years of learning to be anonymous in crowds. He glanced around and realised he had everyone's attention. 'But, I haven't finished yet.'

The man's face remained impassive, but his eyes softened. He leaned in. 'Listen, comrade, if the manager Arianna were here you could stay, but...' His head nodded toward the large man standing behind the wood-panelled bar at the end. 'He doesn't like our type. Let alone our politics. Take my advice and leave now.'

Indignant at the request, Gigi jumped up and turned around. He swung his arms out wide in protest. His chair clattered to the ground. The soft carpet that ran down the middle of the cafe absorbed most of the sound, but that was irrelevant as an old lady screamed something about the Red Brigades and a wave of panic consumed the patrons.

Adrenaline shot through Gigi's system, and although he had done nothing wrong, that didn't matter. Being called a terrorist was enough to end up in jail for the night.

The man behind the bar bent down to grab something. A gun?

Gigi had to get out of there. His legs however ignored the demand.

'Freeze!'

A Carabinieri officer stood at the door, his Beretta pistol aimed at Gigi.

He had no idea that Gigi could do little more than comply.

Within a few minutes, Gigi had been marched outside and now stood surrounded by a group of people who had congregated in a semi-circle on the Piazza della Consolata. Their faces a mixture of disgust, support and excitement.

Gigi felt the sharp force of a hand on his back and stumbled forward.

The crowd parted and reformed, unwilling to let their entertainment go.

Under their stares, Gigi looked up toward the statue of the Virgin Mary that rested on top of a nearby column. But instead of seeing his salvation, he heard it.

'Gigi! What is it this time?'

Inspector Cozzi pushed through the onlookers and introduced himself to the Officer before taking charge of the suspect.

'I'm innocent, I swear,' said Gigi, thankful that someone up there had heard his silent prayer. He had known Cozzi for several years, and with each arrest a friendly rapport had been established. The Inspector had always treated him fairly, and while Gigi would never become an informant, heaven forbid, he would share a smoke with the man.

The Inspector led Gigi to a marked Giulia 1600 Super and put him in the back before returning to speak to the arresting officer. The two men talked, laughed, and then spoke with the staff before separating.

After getting into the driver's seat, the Inspector leaned around and explained the situation.

'What! I only knocked over a chair.'

'I know, but the barman is pushing for vandalism. Not to mention the talk of the Red Brigades has everyone on edge. Don't worry, I'll process you quickly and you'll be out by dinner, but the Chief wants to be seen as tough on terrorism. "Show people we have control of the streets," he told us. Sorry Gigi, it's a case of the wrong place, wrong time.'

Gigi slumped back in his seat. His stomach grumbled at the injustice as he was driven to the station for another mark on his record.

Running on Fumes

My head sinks into the luxurious headrest of the Alfetta and I allow the soft leather to cradle me. I close my eyes and surrender to the soothing purr of the car's idling engine. A smile breaks out over my face as my thoughts drift to how far I've come in such a short space of time.

When I stepped out of San Vittore prison twenty-four hours ago, people knew me as Gigi the loser. A professional burglar. And not a successful one at that. I was living proof that crime didn't pay. Still, my most recent trip away gave me space to think, learn new skills and make some new friends. Powerful ones with useful contacts on the outside. Not only did they help me out by arranging a lift back to Torino, but they also hooked me up with a place to stay and a job that paid cash in hand. Starting the next day. Things were looking up and so, of course, with the promise of an immediate payday, I celebrated my luck until closing time.

If it hadn't been for the shards of light penetrating through the cracks of the wooden shutters, who knows at what time I'd have woken? Thankfully, it was summer, and the sun's first rays had done me a favour.

I stumbled out of bed, splashed water over my dry face, ignoring the redness circling my eyes, and threw on some clean clothes. Almost ready, I tossed three cups of bitter coffee down my throat and raced out the door.

Within seconds, the heat hit me, and my temples throbbed. Despite feeling as if my head was in a vice, and my stomach churning its contents round like a washing machine, I continued down the pavement, ignoring every croissant and pastry that called out to me, offering sweet relief.

Rejecting their aromatic delights was painful, and I could practically taste their flaky pastry on my lips, but it was important that I made a good impression on my new colleagues. After all, someone had vouched for me. When you worked in a profession that doesn't allow for a CV, then reputation and references are all you have. Thankfully, I was known in the city as a skilled, if rather unlucky, commercial burglar, but why I told the people inside I was also an accomplished getaway driver, I don't know. Still, it was too late to put the record straight, and when I think about it, I can steal and I can drive, so what more was there to it than that?

As my worries preoccupied me, the minutes flew past and by the time I checked my cheap wristwatch, I realised I'd been trodding the streets for almost an hour. Standing on a dusty pavement, I threw my hands up and sighed. One car, that's all I had to get. Maybe I really was a loser if I couldn't even do that in a city with a bloody *Fiat* factory in it.

At that realisation, my feet ached, my shoulders sagged, and I noticed the foul odour that rose from the damp patches under my armpits. I exhaled and looked round at the sea of vehicles. All unobtainable without getting myself pinched.

Reality kicked at my heart. You can't fight fate. My luck, and with it seemingly my employment, was going to end just as quickly as it started.

Resigned to failure, I slouched around the corner of Via Giulia di Barolo and found myself at a wide intersection on the Corso S.

Maurizio. I glanced about, hoping to see a bar. My stomach was still turning, but now for a different reason. One that only a *caffè corretto* could help. I needed something with a bit of edge to give me the courage to return home.

Then my eyes widened. It was as if God himself had taken pity on me.

Down the road, parked next to a petrol pump, was a brand new Alfa Romeo. The driver's side door was open, the keys were in the ignition, and, unlike in the other streets, there wasn't a single person in sight.

I edged my way down the pavement, past the shuttered windows and doors, and beyond the graffitied flaking walls of the apartment building. The attendant's booth was empty. A small sign in the window said they'd be back in fifteen minutes.

With a final furtive glance, I flung myself towards the vehicle, and in a matter of seconds I was hurtling down the street, racing to pick up my two associates.

Normally, I'm pretty punctual. You need to be in my line of work, as fine margins can be the difference between success and failure. Freedom and incarceration. But on this one occasion, I didn't think it a big deal that I was a little late. My colleagues clearly thought otherwise, and we spent the entire journey in silence.

It didn't bother me much, though, as my mind was on other things. After this job, I would have everything. Money. Women. A new nickname. The possibilities were endless. I had reinvented myself.

I parked up outside the bank, and the two killjoys jumped out of the vehicle and went to work. Alone, I allowed myself the luxury of a quick break. I had earned it. I shut my eyelids and let the gentle hum of the car engine massage my sore head.

***

The roar of gunfire perforates my eardrums. I jerk up in my seat and swing my head from side to side trying to remember where I am. I rub a moist palm down my face and exhale. It's time to earn my money.

As I rev the engine, my mouth feels parched, and a tingling sensation runs through my body. I grip the thin, leather-covered steering wheel. The soft grain caresses my calloused hands, calming my nerves. Momentarily, at least.

I'm still checking everything when my associates fling open the passenger doors and jump in screaming, 'Go! Go! Go!'

Now, sweat is cascading down and off my nose like a waterfall. The once smooth steering wheel sticks to my clammy palms. My body shakes and I tell myself it's the adrenalin. Not nerves. No, not nerves. My breathing becomes shallow. The sides of the car close in on me. I *had* stolen an Alfetta and not a Fiat 500, hadn't I?

A cacophony of sounds fills the metal contraption. My colleagues are still shouting, a siren wails in the distance, and my heart is pounding like a drum. I want to cover my ears and block it all out, but I stay strong, shove the gear stick into first, and release the clutch. The car whines in protest at its treatment but gives in as we shoot out into the sparse traffic. I'm roaring with laughter. But it doesn't last.

My voice jumps an octave higher as the exhaust blows and the car shakes. I jerk forward and my chest bounces off the steering wheel. The muscles in my shoulders go into spasm and a grenade goes off inside my head. My face contorts as the stench of petrol fills my nostrils, and a black smoke drifts over. Covering us in a fog of defeat.

As we roll to a stop, the men in the back are glowering at me. I just know it. There is a lump in my throat. I swallow hard. And again. No one says anything. Through bleary eyes, I glance down at the petrol gauge. The tach needle is in the red.

Shit.

I'm still Gigi the loser.

137 Words to Salvation

The barrage of insults pins me to my chair. I try shifting my weight from one ass cheek to the other, but the hard wooden seat refuses to offer any comfort. Just like my opponent, who continues to spew verbal diarrhoea in my direction.

As he reels off insult after insult, spittle gathers at the corners of his mouth, and he reminds me of a rabid dog going in for the kill. At the mention of my late mother, my cheek turns slightly and I grimace. That one hurt.

Keep it together Gigi.

I force my mind to wander. To seek a distraction. Beneath the refrained chuckling of the crowd, I sense the music of Battisti. But his words of encouragement are lost amongst the fracas.

Out of the corner of my eye, I see the rubberneckers. Their smiles and sneers. I can't blame them. I'd be the same in their shoes. But I'm not. Their drinks slosh as the stinging barbs keep piercing my heart. They keep laughing while I silently pray that the thickening fug of the pool hall will snake its way into my abuser's throat and suffocate him.

It could happen.

The man across from me leans forward. His cheeks puff out and are flushed red. He's on his last legs. His saliva has turned into a near-crusty white froth.

He hurls one more insult at me, then looks around. Chin up. Smug.

'Now, it's Gigi's turn,' the referee announces.

I sit up straight, roll my shoulders, and take a deep breath.

'Stronzo, cabbage head, piss ant, dickhead, coglione, cretin, shit, cock sucker, peckerhead, dork, idiot, fool, clown, buffoon, asshole, bastard, prick, bead-rattler, barbone, clod, coward, imbecile, mook, bag of piss, punk, putz, goon, asslicker, fink, lug, peasant, signora, baby, minchione-' the words flow without conscious thought. I witness my opponent's face shifting, taking the form of everyone that's ever done me wrong. I continue. '-doofus, donkey, dag, jerk, johnson, impotent, chicken, ciuccione, scum, shaveling, deadbeat, dummy, ding-dong, yokel, scab, fruitcake, fennel, pizzle, tool, square, pirla, puke, louse, turncoat, windbag, hophead, bonehead, cuckold-' My throat burns, and I swear someone has shoved a load of cotton balls into my mouth. Every movement of my jaw is a herculean effort. The stale air dries out my throat. Then I see his piggy eyes roll. '-dirty rat, roach, dig, turd, meatball, turkey, bullcat, hound dog, skunk, crud, slime, bedwetter, snot nose.'

Spent, I exhale, letting my lungs recover for a second before I slip a cigarette between my lips and light it. The sweet nicotine calms the washing machine churning in my stomach. I glance at the judge. My hammering heart drowns out the nearby chatter, the smashing of cues on balls, and the distant shouts over suspiciously dealt hands. I puff on my cig and turn to my opponent.

His face is still flushed, but there is an expectant look underneath the tomato complexion. He's no stranger to false hope.

'The priest, 125. Gigi the loser, 137 insults without stopping.'

I expel a plume of smoke up into the air. It feels cathartic.

'Gigi the loser is the winner.'

In one swift move, I toss the cigarette to the floor, stamp it out and lean toward the dome-headed clergyman. I hold out my hand.

His movements are slow and languid, as you'd expect from a man carrying a few extra pounds around the waist. He withdraws a few notes from his pocket. My fingers tingle as they touch the cash.

I can't resist. 'And ball breaker!' Electricity jolts through me and I jump up.

As I walk past the dispersing crowd, random men pat me on the back. They, too, have won money from my performance. I feel like a rock star. One in need of a drink.

Carlo approaches me as I move past the pool tables. First, he offers his congratulations and then an opportunity. Did I want to make some dough doing the sort of work I used to do? I entertain the idea, but only for a moment. It's doing stuff like that which gave me my nickname. I tell him no; I already have a job. Besides, breaking and entering? That's two years and three months. I really need that drink.

I sit at the bar alone. The warm J&B slides down my throat. I should only have the one. Tomorrow, I need to be up at the crack of dawn to peddle watermelons. I wonder if Carlo is still here.

A Real Pizza Work

Standing in the darkness under a broken streetlamp, Gigi put a cigarette into his mouth and stared at the run-down pizzeria across the road. Just like he'd done every night since it happened.

Even though he'd lived opposite the building for over two decades, he'd never really paid any attention to it. Now, though, he'd studied each crack in the wall, learned the words of every advert in the window, and more importantly knew the exact minute when the owner, the odious Francesco Grasso, locked up and left for the evening. The mere thought of that man waddling home, oblivious to the struggles of others, was enough to make Gigi's blood boil.

As Gigi recalled the fateful event, his jaw tightened and his teeth ground together. The evening hadn't started very well. There was little conversation around him and only a warm beer and a cold pizza in front of him. But he was still thankful to be included in the family gathering. Since losing his job and having to support himself by less legal means, invitations like this were rare. So, when Francesco had made an inappropriate advance on his young niece, Gigi couldn't resist making a smart comment at the pizza man's expense. It got some laughs from his family.

Five minutes later though, he had to pick himself off the rough concrete outside the restaurant, spit the gravel out of his mouth, and retreat to his cramped, lonely apartment with his tail between his legs.

In his mind, Gigi could still hear the jeering and laughing that followed him home. Not to mention the muted snivelling of his mother and the ashamed apologies of his cousins.

It was at that moment Gigi cursed Francesco and swore revenge.

Now he was ready.

Not in the sense that he had a plan, but because he knew the restaurant would be closed tomorrow, and it would take Francesco two days to even realise anything had happened.

Francesco. Just the name of the man caused Gigi to clench his jaw, snapping the cigarette in two. Within seconds, the filter had worked itself down his throat, causing him to choke. He flailed his arms and barked out in desperation, stopping only when he doubled over and regurgitated the offending item.

Using the sleeve of his trench coat, he wiped away the saliva that had congealed around his chin and glanced up and down the street. Feeling secure in the night's silence, he cleared his throat and returned to glaring at the restaurant. His right hand drifted to the side pocket of his coat and patted it. He smiled as his fingers touched the small metallic protrusions poking out from under the fabric. It was his key to getting even.

After checking his watch, Gigi rushed across the street and positioned himself at the corner of the alleyway that ran around the building and led to its rear entrance. He lingered there until he heard the slamming of the pizzeria's front door, upon which he retreated into the dark recess, ducking behind an overflowing steel dumpster, then peering out and waiting for Francesco to wobble past.

The night had turned frigid, and as he huddled up against the cold metal, dirt and dust particles irritated his nostrils, causing his shoulders to hunch. His eyelids closed, and his lips squeezed together.

Heavy footsteps echoed around him but rather than prepare for his moment, Gigi clamped his fingers to the bridge of his nose.

As the impulse to sneeze subsided, he opened his eyes in the nick of time to glimpse the pizza chef jiggling past the end of the alley.

This was it.

Gigi scurried to the back door of the pizzeria, slid the lock-pick set out of his pocket, and studied each tool one by one until he found the right one. A slim tension wrench. Armed and ready he got to work on the lock.

The gentle scratching pierced the night, the sound like nails down a chalkboard.

A fine mist of sweat gathered on his forehead. The seconds stretched into agonising hours until a metallic click snapped time back to its normal pace, and the bolt sprang free.

Gigi made the sign of the cross and gave praise for the one blessing he'd received in life.

He stole a look down the alleyway, making sure he was alone. A wave of relief washed over him. He wrapped his hand around the door handle and went to enter.

A dull thud echoed inside Gigi's skull as his forehead smashed into the hard unmoving wooden door, and his vision blurred. His throat felt like it was closing up and his eyes narrowed, desperately trying to stem the tide of tears rising behind them. He shook his head, his muscles tensed, and he emitted a low growl. This was another injustice caused by Francesco. Gigi had let him win again.

He shot a seething glare at the entrance. No one and nothing would stand in his way. With all his force, he bundled forwards, slamming his shoulder against the stiff door.

The wooden frame rattled and the hinges creaked as the door burst open, and Gigi tumbled into the kitchen area, his momentum sending him straight into a shelf laden with tinned tomato sauce.

As the tins hit the tiled floor, a sharp popping sound reverberated through the room. Gigi ducked down and threw his hands around his head to protect himself from this unexpected gunfire. He kept his head covered for a minute and remained unaware of the burst lids spilling out their pungent red goo all over the white tiles around him. Once the noise had subsided, and the butterflies in his stomach settled, he let out his breath, removed a pocket torch, and inspected the space.

His nose twitched as it tried to resist an acrid stench that hung in the air. One which overpowered the spicy aroma of tomato arising from beneath him. His threadbare shoes splashed through the sauce as he searched for the origin of the odour.

As he passed several boxes of ingredients, he racked his brains thinking about what he could steal or do to the place. There was little demand for canned goods on the black market, and swapping the salt and pepper contents around didn't seem to do justice to what he had endured. He was just about to water down the olive oil when he saw it.

He'd hit the jackpot.

A pile of American cigarettes lay on the counter ahead of him. As his torchlight illuminated them, their cellophane wrappers gleamed like beacons of luck. Why hadn't he thought of it before? Everyone in Torino knew Francesco had a contact who smuggled in foreign goods without paying tax but said nothing as they preferred low prices to the moral high ground. Now, it was Gigi's turn to profit. It wasn't just the money that excited him; whoever Francesco reported to would give him a good kicking if this contraband disappeared.

Gigi smiled, unzipped his jacket, and shoved three multi-packs inside. Their tops poked out of his collar, jabbing his substantial chin upwards. He repositioned himself and reached out to grab another handful, but a sharp table corner caught him under the ribcage and dug into his flesh. He cried out as his body contorted, forcing the cigarette packets further into his face. He needed a new plan.

Cursing under his breath, he stumbled around the kitchen, eventually pulling down the nearest large box. He tore it open and tipped its contents out onto the floor.

Lost in his own excitement, he paid no attention to the dull thuds as bag after bag burst on impact with the ground, creating a flour beach that buffered up against the flowing sea of tomato underneath him. Pulse racing, he returned to the cigarettes and shoved as many as he could into the large container. He licked his dry lips as the boxes landed on top of each other. All thoughts of risk had vanished, replaced by fantasies of the cash he was going to make selling the cartons out on the street.

A streak of light cut through the doorway that led to the front of the restaurant and caught Gigi in the face.

He froze.

The sound of a key rattling in the lock of the main door filled the empty restaurant. A series of voices followed it. Shit, why had Francesco returned? Who was with him?

A sudden cold overtook Gigi, and his stomach twisted and turned. The only thing that could be worse than being caught was what might happen afterwards.

The entrance door slammed shut, snapping Gigi out of his daze. Adrenalin flooded his body. He grabbed the box, now overflowing with packs of cigarettes, and bolted out into the alleyway. Glancing over his shoulder and realising no one was following, he continued home.

With a slight moan, he flopped onto the battered brown leather armchair in the front room, the box settling in his lap, and grinned. His focus shifted towards his loot, and he roared with laughter as he pulled out pack after pack, seeing lire instead of cigarettes.

But before he had the chance to count the cartons, his front door rattled violently.

His heart pounded like a jackhammer as he approached and looked through the peephole. Standing there, almost blocking out the light of the hallway, was the corpulent figure of Francesco, with two menacing henchmen in his shadow.

'Open up, Gigi. We know you're in there, and what you've done. You've been caught red-footed,' said Francesco with a crooked smile. 'Don't make us do this the hard way. I might enjoy it a little too much.'

Ready to protest his innocence, Gigi wiped his clammy hands down the sides of his trousers, took a deep breath, and prepared to open the door. His hand hovered over the handle as he contemplated the sight at his feet: the red and white footprints that he'd tracked into the flat.

His face matched the sauce.

The Card Sharps

I looked him dead in the eye. My stomach churned with the fear of losing everything, but I kept my facial muscles still. No, it wasn't anxiety making me feel this way. It had to be that joint I smoked an hour ago. Yeah, that was it.

The long, thin fluorescent bulb above flickered, turning the worn green felt that separated us into a dark abyss. I was grateful for the respite from the intense scrutiny of his black, beady eyes.

As the light buzzed back to life, the gambling den and its menagerie of well-dressed people, partly obscured by too much cigarette and cigar smoke, returned.

I tensed my jaw and sized up my victim once more. He was nothing. Naïve. Alone. Barely twenty, dressed in designer gear and throwing his parents' money around like confetti. The perfect mark. Now, cards had never been my game, and I was only doing this as a favour for a pal in a fix, but even I could take this sucker with little effort.

The kid flashed an arrogant smirk. I let him think it was unsettling me. But I held a secret. One that, if played right, would guarantee me the winnings. Well, half of them anyway.

'Are you going to play or fold?'

His voice was whiney, with a hint of insistence. He'd been trying to hurry me along all game.

I rocked on my heels and stole a look at the bearded man hovering over my opponent's shoulder. The situation was perfect. Whenever my adversary peeked at his cards, so did he.

'I'm considering my move,' I said, stalling.

The young man tapped his foot impatiently on the hardwood floor. I jerked my head up. The sound annoyed me.

I cleared my throat and grabbed the beer that was patiently waiting for me on the corner of the table. The smooth liquid went down easy. A bonus.

This latest delay made him check his cards again. More out of boredom that anything, I imagined, but as he looked, so did my man beside him.

I inhaled the alcohol fumes and the cigarette stench that surrounded us, while the bearded man scratched his cheek with two fingers. His thumb jutted out behind the jaw.

I nodded subtly, but immediately cursed myself. A seasoned player would have seen through this charade, but thankfully not this entitled jackass in front of me.

With a sniff, the rich boy turned to face the spectator, but before speaking, the man raised his hands in apology and stepped back.

Idiot. It took all my self-control to stop from breaking out into a grin.

The mark huffed before refocusing on the game and myself. His eyes bored into me. Fuck. Did he suspect? I didn't actually smile, did I? Worried, I feigned interest in my cards and dropped my gaze. This game was all about waiting, and normally I could be very patient. As a burglar I had to be, but when I'd had a drink and got in a place like this, something came over me. I told myself to hold it together and wait. Just a little longer. It was the same situation with my lovemaking, sadly.

A sudden cough shattered the tension. The time to earn my keep had arrived.

My partner – let's be honest, that's what he was tonight – was now bent over double, taking the mark with him as he coughed up a lung. He sold it well. A thirty-a-day habit certainly helped him get into character.

Sweat poured down my back. Why? Perhaps the heating had been turned up. This sort of place played these tricks in order to get people to drink more. Or maybe it was because I was standing under the relentless buzz of the blazing light. It had recovered from its earlier laziness and decided to make up for it by shining brighter than the sun. I narrowed my eyes and a pain shot through my head. The room spun, and my mouth became dry. I forced myself to resist grabbing the bottle of beer nearby. Instead, I slid a hand behind my back and sought the right card.

My fingertips traced the subtle creases at the top left corner of each card tucked into my belt. If only I could recall their meanings. Thankfully, the one I wanted was on the right. But was my right or my opponents?

Sweat stung my eyes, causing the other patrons to blur. Their shapes were barely distinguishable from the mottled green wallpaper that wrapped around this den of iniquity.

My eyes flicked towards my companion's face. Seeking solace.

He was too busy pushing that lung back down his throat.

Alone, I couldn't move. My right hand hovered behind me.

A glass shattered in the distance. The sound kick-starting my mind, and I pulled myself together.

In that heartbeat, I yanked at the card from behind my back and tossed it onto the green baize, just as the original one slid down my sleeve.

My accomplice had recovered and now the mark had, with increased visible annoyance, returned his attention to me.

The light above and everything else in the place died. An eerie silence fell over the premises. No clinking of glasses. No jovial cheers. Nothing.

All three of us stared at the card, brows furrowed, trying to decipher the significance.

It took a moment but I realised the problem and looked up just in time to see my opponent halfway across the table. His fist grew ever bigger.

The five aces on the table weren't the only thing that was laid flat out.

In a Real State

'Coffee?' said Antonio, lowering his own cup.

'It'd be rude to say no,' said Gigi. In truth he was grateful for the offer, as money had been in short supply since he'd been released from prison.

He took a stool at the marble counter next to his childhood friend, who raised a finger towards the barista and ordered another drink.

After a cursory smile at each other, the two men sat in silence as they waited. Both faced forward, pretending to be interested in the shiny La Marzocco espresso machine that took up much of the space behind the counter. The sharp hiss of steam and rhythmic hum of extraction filled the void in conversation. And although Gigi was glad for something to concentrate on, rather than having to make awkward small talk, he was also grateful for being able to take a moment and appreciate the little things.

It had never bothered him before, but during that last stretch inside he'd been surprised to discover what he missed. The anticipation and enjoyment of a good coffee was one of them. The thrill of his work was another. He sighed. How many times had they put him away now? Crime never paid, at least not for him.

When he'd stepped out of those gates, he decided it was time to go straight. To say goodbye to the adrenalin rush that had seen him lose so much of his life. He had to become responsible and carve out a safe, sensible life for himself.

From the corner of his eye, he glanced at Antonio. Although they shared a bond born of adolescent adventure and poverty, he'd been a kid who was going places. He had brains and morals, unlike the rest of the tenement. Had Gigi stuck with him back then, his life would have been completely different. Too late now, though.

His gaze dropped to the empty counter in front of him. Had the silence gone on for too long? Someone had to say something soon.

Moments later, to Gigi's relief, the barista placed a filled porcelain cup and a saucer on the counter. After he'd thanked them both, he inhaled the sweet, almost fruity aroma rising from the coffee. He lifted the cup, and as the edge of the warm porcelain touched his lips, Antonio broke the silence.

'No sugar?'

'Stopped years ago,' said Gigi, before taking a sip and placing the cup down.

'I've not seen you around for a while. You been away?' asked Antonio, twisting his body to face his friend.

Gigi noticed the strain in Antonio's voice and the bags under his moist eyes.

'In a manner of speaking. Nowhere nice, though, before you ask. Anyway, what about you? How are you keeping?'

'You remember Maria Assunta?'

'Your school sweetheart, wasn't she?'

'Yeah. Married her last month. Kid on the way,' said Antonio with a flicker of a smile.

At the mention of a child, Gigi's thoughts turned inward. His eyes flickered with visions of past mistakes and a future that never was. His shoulders slumped, and he picked up the cup to hide the movement.

To let the moment pass. 'I didn't know. Congratulations. When's it due?'

'In two months.'

'Oh. Is that why you look...' he said, returning the cup to the saucer.

Antonio laughed before his face tightened and turned serious. 'No. We've dealt with that issue. Kind of. We were about to move into a new apartment this week, and despite this ... this scandal, things were going OK, but then I got fired from the factory. I joined one strike – one! – and they said I was a commie agitator. I gave that company five years of my life, and they couldn't even give me a day's notice. Nothing. Then Vanni, you know him? The estate agent based out of Parco Dora. Well, he came round to my parents' house the same day. Lord knows how he knew what happened. He told me I couldn't have the place anymore unless I had a job. That we'd be better off moving to China.' Antonio hit the counter with his palm and looked away.

Gigi's cup and saucer rattled at the impact. He shook his head at the story before gulping down the rest of his coffee. Ideology. It ruined everything.

'You want to know the worst part? Worse than that, I mean,' said Antonio. 'He said the deposit was non-refundable. We'd paid a month in advance, too. Over a hundred and fifty thousand lire! Now, what are we going to do?'

'So, you're telling me you have no money, and you still bought me a coffee?'

'Of course.'

'You can't afford to be buying people drinks just because they turn up somewhere.' The dull ache of guilt spread around the back of Gigi's skull. He pushed the thought away and gritted his teeth. It would have been worse for him to pay.

'I've already broken one unwritten rule. I'm not about to break another.'

Gigi smiled and nodded. That was true. Some societal rules needed to be followed. 'Tell you what, come back here at eight thirty tomorrow morning and I'll repay the favour.' Then he got up and headed towards the door.

'Where you going?'

'To get ready for work,' said Gigi, without looking back.

***

The next morning, Gigi sat in the same place as the day before, ordered an almond croissant with a cappuccino, and waited. By the time Antonio arrived, Gigi had finished his breakfast, read the pink sports newspaper *Gazzetto dello Sport,* and weathered the disapproving look of the barista when he requested a *caffè corretto*. The touch of grappa added to his coffee was the perfect pick-me-up after a night shift.

Antonio stumbled in wearing an extra day's stubble and plopped down on the stool next to Gigi. He rubbed a hand down his face and nodded at the barista, who glanced across as he served another customer further down the bar.

'Rough night?' said Gigi, stifling a yawn. His friend looked as he felt, but he couldn't say that.

'Maria and I had this big fight, and...,' said Antonio, flicking out a hand.

'That's OK. I'm sure things will improve for you both soon.' Seeing the lack of belief on his friend's face, Gigi continued, 'I got your money back from Vanni, and a little extra for your inconvenience.'

Antonio blinked at Gigi, then tilted his head as his eyebrows squished together, forming a monobrow. 'What? How?' The wooden stool beneath him wobbled.

'Well, let's just say I didn't get a receipt for it,' said Gigi with a smile as he remembered the tingling sensation that had coursed through his fingers as they manipulated the simple lock on the office door and the satisfaction in beating a basic safe. Although he'd thought he might be rusty, he had managed it all in record time.

He noticed his friend was staring at him. 'Best you keep the news to yourself, though,' he said, as his left foot pushed a small duffel bag across the floor towards Antonio. 'One more thing. I need you to pay for my breakfast.'

To Kill a Prosecutor

As Enzo plucked the half-smoked cigarette from his mouth and tossed it to the pavement, his eyes remained fixed on the first-floor apartment. After two weeks of enduring the freezing northern mornings, he'd finally been confident enough to make his move. He thought the prosecutor operated like clockwork. Only now, the clock had stopped.

He blew out a plume of smoke and looked down the still-sleepy Torinese street of Via Lamarmora, before crushing the butt's dying embers under his heel.

Then, with a leather-gloved hand, he rolled up his jacket sleeve and checked his watch. It was five past seven.

His mind ran through the sequence that should have unfolded. On a Sunday, the prosecutor should have raised the external green blinds covering the kitchen window at six forty-five. Then at seven, his wife and young daughter would appear for their family breakfast. Just over an hour later, they'd all leave in their unarmoured Giulietta, driving out through the side gate on Via Governolo, and take a fifteen-minute drive to the Chiesa di Santa Maria del Monte dei Cappuccini.

That was his window of opportunity. It was the only journey the prosecutor ever took without bodyguards.

Yet today, the family slept in. It could have been nothing. A faulty alarm clock, maybe. Attending a later service. Or perhaps someone had squealed. Whatever the reason, it complicated matters.

Enzo knew from bitter experience that if the first two actions were missed, then the third was unlikely to happen. He ran his tongue over the front of his top teeth and considered his next move.

In the distance, the sounds of motor vehicles grew and, despite this affluent area of Crocetta still being quiet, if he spent any longer hanging around, the locals would notice. He doubted it would take much for these people of power, or at least ambition, to call the police if they deemed an undesirable had infiltrated their secure little quarter. And, with everything going on in the city, let alone the country, they would be right to do so.

By now, he'd wasted a couple more minutes standing and thinking instead of acting. The frigid air pierced his lungs, and the chill had filled his cheeks and all but frozen his teeth.

Sighing with acceptance, he hunched his neck down, popped up the faux-fur-lined collar of his jacket and dug his leather gloves deep into its side pockets. Then he headed down the road, across the pedestrian crossing and down the adjacent Via Governolo, pausing only to look at the vehicle gate of the prosecutor's building.

He continued past the rows of parked cars and unremarkable residential buildings until he reached the end of the street, where he turned right onto Corso Galileo Ferraris and approached an idling Fiat 238 van which was decorated with a sprayed-on sign for the Tuscan shaving company Proraso.

After checking up and down the empty street, he pulled open the side door and clambered in. Dried sweat and stale tobacco immediately hit him in the face and caused his nose to twitch. He sniffed as he sat down on a modified bench seat that ran the length of the back and nodded at the driver, Daniele, who glanced over his pink sports newspaper to check the rear-view mirror.

After peeling off his gloves, Enzo placed them next to him and rubbed his hands together. When he was satisfied that he'd warmed up, he retrieved a tiny black notebook and pencil from the left pocket of his jeans. The tools of his trade. The non-lethal ones, anyway. He recorded that morning's observations, noting each detail with the gravity of a chess player plotting their next move.

He remained sitting there, thinking over the anomaly, and accepted the plan was no longer viable. The reason was irrelevant. The indictment was scheduled for tomorrow, and he had strict instructions not to let that happen. They had given him two weeks to pull off this job, and he wanted to make sure he lived to tell the tale. A target of such importance required patience and understanding. It needed more planning. But Enzo doubted whether his bosses would see it that way.

He swallowed down the lump in his throat, put down the pad and pencil, and took a series of slow deep breaths. Feeling more relaxed, he reached under the bench and pulled out a small hard polypropylene case, which he rested on his lap. He unclipped the catches and retrieved a Benelli B76 pistol and a suppressor, which he attached, checked over and then disassembled, placing it beside him on top of the gloves.

'We can't risk waiting any longer,' he said. He needed this to go well and not just because of the immediate deadline. If he made this hit, they would promote him to the rank of *Santista* and welcome him into the major society of the *'Ndrangheta*. He was fortunate that a recent kidnapping had gone wrong, leading to a shoot-out, a crackdown, and an unexpected opening for a new *capo*.

The other bosses had recognised that Enzo differed from other *camorrista di sgarro*. For his peers, the extra money and clout brought about by this promotion would excite them, perhaps even make them more arrogant and reckless, but Enzo had built a reputation for efficiency and reliability. This was his career and a way to drag his family out of poverty. A chance to ensure his little one wouldn't need to scrape a living on the farms or, worse, by kidnapping and killing like he'd done.

Behind the wheel, Daniele folded up his paper, tossed it onto the front passenger seat, looked into the rear mirror again, and killed the engine. 'You waited too long. You sure you can do it?'

The impertinence caused Enzo's teeth to grind together. He picked up the pistol and turned to face his assistant. Who was he to doubt his plans? That fresh-faced *picciotto* had not yet been a member of the society for a year and needed to learn his place.

'Your job is to drive, not question. The prosecutor only leaves the house without an escort on Sunday. Straight to Mass and back again. The idiot believes even bodyguards should have the holy day off. That was the logical time to do it. But if he doesn't leave, and he won't today, I'll have to go in. There's no other choice now.'

'Collateral damage?'

Enzo nodded before picking up a 9mm Luger cartridge and feeding it into the pistol. The click filled the silence. He then withdrew the magazine, pushed in another round, to replace the one that fed into the chamber, and reloaded. Next he positioned the weapon in his shoulder holster beneath his jacket and pocketed the suppressor.

He had nine bullets. And potentially three people to take out. Although he hoped not. He'd never faced a situation that required him to sanitise a woman or child before. This was supposed to be a simple job. He and Daniele had been sent up north to solve a single problem. Not to kill a family. One like his. His personal misgivings weren't important, though. This was business, and his deadline was due. Failure was not an option. He knew that if the countdown on the prosecutor ran out, then one would start on him. No promotion. No future.

'Give me that picture again,' said Enzo.

Daniele tore off the black-and-white photograph of the prosecutor that was taped to the dashboard and passed it back over his shoulder.

Enzo took the image, familiarising himself one last time with the target before returning it to the driver. 'I'll go in. Clean up and get out. Then we head straight for Calabria.'

Daniele shoved the photo into the glovebox of the van and grunted a reply.

Biting his cheek, Enzo hoped the kid could hold his nerve and not leave him out in the cold. Yet he had no choice but to trust his integrity and mettle. 'When you circle the block, find a cafe and call the boss. Tell him the new plan, but do it in code. *Capisci*?'

'Sure,' said Daniele, waving a hand in acknowledgment as he watched Enzo push open the door and step out into the bright, frosty morning.

***

Gigi put the torch on the smooth, cold surface of the marble kitchen top next to the scrunched up high-visibility jacket that he'd tossed there earlier, after his initial search of the apartment.

He then sat down on a grotesque modern-art bar stool and with hands covered by thin latex gloves withdrew the small lock-picking set that was tucked away in his trouser pocket and then pulled out a crumpled letter with his instructions on it.

As he looked at the tools, a tingling sensation ran up the back of his neck. There was something about this job that made him feel uneasy.

Early last night in his local pool hall, a thin man nicknamed Spaghettino had approached him and shoved a down payment of two million lire into his hands. It was more than he'd earned all year and impossible to refuse.

One beer later and he gave his word that he was in. He asked some basic questions, naturally, but in his inebriated state, it sounded like an easy payday. All he had to do was access a residential apartment the next morning and steal some documents from a home office. Spaghettino had even written it all down for him.

It was only when he already inside, walking down the hallway, and saw the framed portrait staring at him that he realised he'd forgotten to ask who the mark was. The piercing eyes of the famed Prosecutor Sarri challenged him to complete the theft. This was a man who took a no-nonsense approach to applying the law, and because of this, had several people gunning for him. Literally.

Gigi berated himself for not taking a bit more care. No matter the situation, a professional should have cased the joint, understood the comings and goings of occupants, and more importantly devised his own plan, but there'd not been time. And he wasn't being paid to do that. Just to follow instructions.

He'd thought of none of that of course when he woke up, bleary-eyed and with a headache at six that morning. Or thirty minutes later when he accessed the building using a fraudulent bank card to loid the lock on the entrance door.

From then on, it was a simple case of working a pick and a tension tool to unlock the deadbolt on the apartment door and then slide inside. The result of such efficiency was that there was little time to think about what he'd got himself into.

Before he knew it, he'd performed his usual walkthrough of the location and ditched the fluorescent workman's jacket he wore for these types of jobs. He always found it amazing that such a bright piece of clothing seemed invisible to the middle and upper classes. Of course, if anyone ever looked closely and saw his tattered jeans or thin canvas trainers, they might ask questions. But they never did. As a result, that form of urban camouflage was perfect for any daytime job.

But now, sitting alone in the kitchen, Gigi had the time to worry. He glanced at the letter again, re-reading that the inhabitants would be gone until at least ten. The deadline caused him to check his watch. Ten-past-seven.

A yawn escaped his mouth, and he stretched his arms out while glancing around the spotless kitchen. It didn't take him long to locate a Moka pot and a packet of Lavazza *Fiera di Milano*.

He loaded up the percolator's filter and took a moment to savour the sweet nutty aroma of the ground coffee, before screwing the top and bottom of the coffeemaker together and placing it on the hob.

While he waited for the magical elixir to bubble out of the spout, he wondered how people functioned at this hour. Early mornings were a killer.

Several minutes later and the pot made a spitting and popping sound as the coffee filled the top chamber of the Moka. Gigi picked it up and rushed towards the sink, cooling its lower half under the tap before drying it and placing it on the countertop, lid up. The scent wafted out, filling the room. He closed his eyes and smiled as his olfactory glands sent a wave of near euphoria through his body.

The peace only lasted a few seconds before his stomach reminded him it was still empty.

He headed across to the gigantic fridge in the corner and had to use all his strength to pull open the twin doors. As they opened, a blast of bright light hit him in the eyes, causing him to blink as the cool air ran along the contours of his face.

He stared at the contents. It was as if he'd entered a supermarket. At the very bottom was a large tray filled with brightly coloured fruits, while cold meats and cheese populated the lower shelves, and an array of jars covered in brand names adorned the upper levels. So, this was what it was like to be rich.

Appreciation over, he whipped up a croissant stuffed with as much salami and cheese as he could squeeze between the bread. He poured a coffee and dumped two heaped teaspoons of sugar in it, before stirring the spoon around and settling down on the same tall stool by the countertop.

After downing the drink, he picked up his croissant, but out of the corner of his eye, he saw the instructions. The thin piece of paper screamed at him in the tone of his old mentor, Moggi.

Gigi lowered the snack and cocked his head. He could hear the gruff, gravelly voice of the old thief, and his most repeated advice, 'in order to be a successful burglar you have to get in and out quickly, leaving no trace'.

A chunk of cheese dropped out of the stuffed pastry and landed with a wet slap on the floor.

He looked at the mess and shrugged, dismissing not only it but also the guidance. That was only relevant when you were unsure about the whereabouts of a security guard or proprietor. As long as he'd been given accurate information, he'd be safe for a few hours. And if he tidied up after himself, no one would ever know anyone had been there. Well, not until they tried to find the documents.

He licked his lips and raised the overflowing pastry to his mouth.

Then the latch on the front door rattled.

***

Enzo gritted his teeth and shook the rake pick inside the apartment door lock. Beads of sweat had formed around his temples, and the strap of his shoulder holster pinched at the clammy skin under his right arm.

With the taste of salt in his mouth, he continued to battle with the stubborn lock. But every rattle of the thin metal instrument screeched like a nail down a chalkboard and his jaw tensed even more. The pain rose into his head, and as the threat of being discovered increased, so did his discomfort.

He swore under his breath. He was a killer, not a burglar. Why couldn't the mark have just stuck to the schedule?

The pick rattled louder and louder until the noise bounced around inside his skull and scraped away at his composure. He withdrew the tool, clenched his fists, and pulled an arm back, ready to strike the door.

A low grunt escaped his closed mouth, but he caught himself before doing anything stupid.

He exhaled, taking the moment to centre himself, before walking in a small circle and shaking out his arms. Soon the tension left his body and the vice that had been squeezing his head released its grip.

Clarity returned to his mind. Getting into the apartment wasn't enough. His entry needed to be silent as well. He was a professional, not some street punk. Anyone can pull a trigger, but not everyone could get away with it.

He checked the corridor and, satisfied no one was around, he placed an ear up against the door.

There was no sound from inside. He'd been lucky.

Then he kneeled, and with his brow furrowed, reinserted the rake pick.

He bounced the pins one by one, and with each click, his smile grew wider. There was never any doubt that he'd succeed. This was why the bosses had selected him.

As the final click sounded out, Enzo straightened up, withdrew his pistol from the holster, and screwed on the suppressor.

Now ready, he held the gun up by his shoulder and reached down with his free hand. His leather-gloved fingers wrapped around the wooden doorknob and turned it to the right.

The door opened with a faint sound, and Enzo stepped inside. He found himself in a hallway that was furnished with two sideboards, a mirror and a portrait of a man who resembled the mark. There was also a series of doors on either side, but only one was open.

He cocked his head as the unmistakable aroma of coffee hung in the air's stillness.

Someone was awake. He prayed it was the target.

After closing the door and leaving it unlocked for a quick exit, he indexed his right finger onto the side of the pistol raised it to shoulder height.

That simple action flicked a switch inside his mind, and he ceased being Enzo. He had never really analysed why he changed at that moment, but figured it was his way of disassociating from the act. Whether that was true was something for the prison shrinks to work out, not him.

His knees bent automatically, and he took three deliberate steps forward.

As he moved, he slowed his breathing and relaxed his muscles. This type of scenario wasn't new to him. He would enjoy the adrenalin rush when he accomplished the kill, but for now, he had to remain focused.

Then a loud metallic clang erupted from beyond the open door.

He'd been made.

***

Sitting on the tall stool, Gigi ignored the salami and cheese sprawled out on the countertop before him and tilted his head. The continuous noise of a lock being forced open consumed his attention.

Most people wouldn't have noticed the low scratching made by a pick. However, his years of experience had honed his ear, increasing his sensitivity and ability to recognise the sounds of his trade, no matter how faint.

As a gentle click sounded out, Gigi twisted his torso, gripped the backrest and swung one leg out, dangling it over the floor. His eyes darted around the kitchen, searching for the best escape route.

Going anywhere via the hallway was out. It might bring him face to face with the new intruder, and any confrontation would certainly see him on the losing side. He didn't carry a gun and was useless in a fist fight. The chances that his opponent would be as incompetent were low.

As his eyes continued to search the kitchen, he considered every possibility. A cupboard? No. The fridge was large enough, but its shelves were packed. Could he still make room? He shook his head. That left him with only one option. Which, when he thought about it, was the most obvious. The wraparound balcony. But would he have time to unlock it?

Decision made, Gigi propelled himself towards the balcony door, sending the angular stool crashing to the ground.

***

Enzo's heavy black boots echoed off the parquet flooring as he shortened the distance between himself and the open door.

Unsure who he was going to find, his stomach tightened as he stormed the room with his pistol raised. His muscles twitched, eager to see action as adrenalin flooded his body. He strained to control his impulses, as his gun moved in a smooth arc and covered the immediate corners with ease. Then he sidestepped across the space and into the centre of the room.

No one.

Enzo's attention turned to the overturned chair and the mess on the nearby table. It was consistent with what he'd expected, but the high visibility jacket sent his mind racing, as he tried to rationalise the item with the surroundings.

He shook his head and ran through every scenario. Was the apartment being renovated? Was that the reason for the change in routine? No. In a confined space like this, there'd be no need for that type of bright protective clothing. It must be something else. Another complication. Another witness?

He glanced around the spacious kitchen. There was very little beyond the thin pieces of modern furniture that all but removed any possibility of concealment, and for that, he was thankful. Then he advanced towards the wide lower cupboards, and one by one flung them open, pointing the barrel at the crockery inside.

With a sigh, he placed his hands on his hips and looked about. Only the ostentatious fridge remained. Surely not.

With his left hand, he wrapped his gloved fingers around the handle of the large, white, buzzing appliance, and with his right, he raised his pistol by the barrel, ready to strike his victim.

As he yanked the door open, he twisted his lower body, pivoting on his lead foot. His trailing shoulder followed, and with it the butt of the gun sliced through the air in a devastating cross punch, smashing into a head of cabbage.

The cruciferous vegetable exploded on impact, sending strands of green flying.

After stepping back and shaking excess leaves from his pistol and his clothing, he took in the devastation and a rare chuckle broke out from his dry throat. He stifled the moment by pressing his lips together and setting his jaw.

His eyes narrowed as he stared at the covered windows and the balcony door. It was the only exit route remaining. He cursed himself for his stupidity and followed it up with a muttered repentance for taking the Lord's name in vain.

Not wanting to waste any more time, he approached the balcony door, reached for the cord that controlled the closed blinds and gripped it hard. A feeling of satisfaction swept over him as he raised the blinds a few inches.

Low beams of light made their way inside. He crouched down and pressed his face against the glass, the brightness of the sun causing him to squint as he attempted to see what or who was out there.

In the bright haze, a slight movement caught his attention. It barely lasted a second, and the shape could have been anything, but Enzo was certain. He had flushed out his prey.

He stood up straight, and with his left hand pressed down the handle of the door, testing its resolve. And although stiff, it yielded to the pressure with little resistance. He allowed it to open just an inch, but enough to let in a cool breeze that did nothing to quell the indeterminable warmth that filled him.

Leaving the door ajar, he, puffed out his chest, and breathed in the smell of victory. Satisfied the job would soon be complete, he strode back across the kitchen into the hallway.

That balcony had to lead somewhere. And that was where he would wait.

***

Gigi's body trembled in the frigid single-digit temperature. His fingers pressed against the cold brick of the building as he peered round the corner. Seeing that no one pursued him, a sigh of relief escaped his mouth and formed a misty cloud before him. Had his luck changed?

He paused for a moment and listened. There was only the faint sound of light traffic.

However, for a man like Gigi, these moments of reflection were not good. He was happiest when he didn't have time to think. For his mind to talk to him about everything that might go wrong. It wasn't paranoia or anxiety telling him these things, but bitter experience.

These thoughts swirled around in his head, and because of that, it took his brain a second longer to register the minor detail that was off. It was only when the sunlight bounced off a piece of exposed window and caused him to squint that he realised the blinds had been raised. Someone was looking for him.

No, that didn't make sense. They would have been after the prosecutor.

The prosecutor had become a bit of a celebrity recently. He was a man who courted the media, and after winning a few high-profile cases, Rome had heralded him as the saviour of society. Not everyone agreed, though, and his anti-mafia crusade was at odds with how the Italian economy actually worked. For that reason, his actions had no doubt struck him off more than a few people's Christmas card lists.

Yes, they must have been here for him. The only problem was he wasn't there. But poor Gigi was. And no one knew that except for Spaghettino. A man who had given no notice for this job, just a load of cash. And an amount promised that, on reflection, was too good to be true. The sort of money you would offer to a patsy, knowing full well you wouldn't have to pay.

At this thought, Gigi's mind went into overdrive as attempts to understand the situation descended into paranoid panic. Had that rat set him up? Was he there to take the fall for a bungled robbery while they got what they wanted?

Gigi shook his head side to side, hoping the physical act would somehow help convince him. It must have been a coincidence. But whatever the truth, whoever had entered the apartment was there for a reason, and it wasn't a friendly chat.

To quieten his internal voices that were growing louder every second, he took action and shuffled towards the kitchen door. He had to know if they were still there. Each step brought a fresh fear, and the doubt that had crept up on him now stomped all over his bravado. What if they were waiting there for him?

The slight click of a pistol carried on the wind during that moment of indecision.

Gigi crouched down instinctively. He had heard that sound before when witnessing mafiosi racking the slide of their pistols. Knowing what it meant, he pivoted and changed direction in one smooth motion. His thighs burned as he powered his way back along the side wall and towards a covered window.

Now positioned underneath it, he glanced out through the metal bars of the balcony railing and checked the still empty street. Then he cautiously straightened up in front of the external blind, allowing his muscles to stretch. The pleasure lasted only a moment as the unexpected exercise strained his hamstrings and they told him in no uncertain terms he needed to take better care of his body.

He grimaced at the discomfort of his burning legs as he pushed the external blind out behind him. Crushed up against the window, he pressed his head close, placed a hand above his eyes and peered into the dark room.

Despite the absence of light inside, he made out the outlines of various objects and recognised it as the second bedroom. His eyes moved over the window frame. An easy wooden thing that anyone could open with minimal fuss, even with its latch. He was thankful that windows this high up rarely had much security, focusing instead on user convenience.

After placing his hands on each vertical frame, he slid the right side up and then the left. It creaked before rising and allowing Gigi to slide his fingers down and underneath. Then he lifted the frame until a sufficiently large gap formed. He exhaled before clambering in sideways. The elevated ridge of the sill pressed into the softness of his midsection, causing him to bite his lower lip.

He fell inside and his right elbow banged against the hard floor, followed by his right shoulder blade, and his body crashed to the ground with a dull thud. Moisture formed around the corners of his eyes and he hissed in pain. After recovering, he slid his back up against the wall, and waited for his eyes to adjust and the aching to subside.

A moment later the previously outlined furniture became clearer. Inside the functional room was a double bed, an enormous wardrobe, and what looked to be a matching chest of drawers. It was tasteful, but not valuable. No wonder he'd paid little attention earlier when looking the place over.

While rubbing his chin with his index finger and thumb, he considered his next move. If the person remained in the apartment, then completing the job would be impossible. The only thing left to do was get out alive. And then consider leaving town for a bit.

He nodded his own acceptance of this simple new plan and shuffled towards the door. There he laid on his stomach, placed his head sideways on the floor, and peered through the gap beneath the door.

As his body squirmed in an attempt to see further up the hallway, his cheek brushed across the hardwood floor, which dragged the skin taut and caused his eyes to narrow as he tried to control the irritation. The effort and pain proved worthless as only an adjacent door, which he guessed was the master bedroom, was visible. Nothing that could help him.

He sat up, rubbed his sore cheek, and considered his options. Waiting in the room was tempting. The wardrobes looked large enough to accommodate him comfortably for a few hours. But then what? The prosecutor and his goons would return, and he'd get nabbed. No, he'd have to go for it. Commit. Words of encouragement drifted from his lips and filled his ears. He was capable. He was a professional burglar, after all. Sneaking around undetected was what he did.

With one palm on the door, he used the other to press down the handle. He held his breath as the latch gave a small click. In the silence, it might as well have been an alarm.

On his tiptoes, he made his way down the hall, past the second bedroom. He continued, reaching an ornate hallway table with a mirror above it. Here, he paused. The hair on his arms and neck raised and a tingling sensation coursed through his body. It was what happened right before the thrill of completing a job.

In just a few more steps, he'd be at the door to the home office. Maybe he could get away with this after all.

His gaze lingered on the door, a gateway to untold riches, before a movement in the mirror stole his attention.

A shadowy figure standing side-on reflected at him. The only thing that appeared real was the long barrelled pistol held up in his right hand.

What sounded like the crack of a whip followed, and Gigi blinked.

His eyes flashed open, wide, just as the air next to his nose split in half and something deep inside his mind told him death was near.

With a thunderous explosion, the mirror shattered, spraying hundreds of tiny shards into the air from where they cascaded onto him.

He ducked down and covered his head. But caught in this deluge of sharp glass, it was too late to stop several fragments from piercing his skin.

'*Cazzo*!' He never thought his voice could reach that high, but the scream released all the nervous tension held within and forced his body into action. Still hunched over, he launched forward, crashing into the office door with a thunderous boom.

Gigi's heart pounded so hard it drowned out everything else as his fingers fumbled with the handle. The seconds it took him to gain purchase felt like hours, and with a maniacal cheer, he shoved the door open and scrambled inside before slamming it shut behind him.

He knew more than anyone that a closed door offered no real protection against someone who wanted in, but it provided enough security to trick his brain into believing the situation wasn't as bad as it was.

As the immediate threat waned, his breaths turned shallow and fast. Comforted by a moment of respite, his mind played through worst-case scenarios. As it did, beads of sweat rolled down his face, stinging as they tracked over all the tiny lacerations.

He bit into his lower lip, controlling the fear, but his body trembled as he pressed an ear against the wooden door.

The sound of quick, heavy footprints resonated through the air, intensifying as they came ever closer.

Then the doorknob rattled violently.

***

Gigi's eyes darted across the office. Now seeing it for the second time that morning, he realised the prosecutor had converted the room from the master bedroom. The presence of an en suite confirmed that.

His next thought was for the poor Signora Prosecutor, who had to be relegated to a smaller bedroom because of her husband's preference for work over their marital relationship. Some men don't deserve wives.

The continued rattling of the handle brought him back to reality, and with a sigh, he began appraising the furniture, not for what each piece could earn him, but for how they could help him survive.

In a matter of seconds, he discarded the large desk that dominated the room and the roll-top desk in the corner. Both would be too heavy to move. The chairs were too light to stop anyone from entering and an array of legal books on the shelves wouldn't fend off someone with a pizza cutter, let alone a gun. His gaze settled on a large, metallic filing cabinet in the near corner.

He scrambled in its direction before wrapping his arms round the object like he was embracing an old friend. The time for sentimentality over, he pivoted and hauled the cabinet towards the door, going from left to right and back again.

Every twist caused his sides to strain, while a guttural noise pushed itself through the gaps of his teeth. The shrill scraping of metallic corners against a polished floor joined his own sounds of desperation while the rhythmic thud of the unit bouncing from side to side underpinned the chaos.

A final bang rang out as the cabinet landed in front of the opening door, keeping the aggressor at bay.

Gigi heard a furious snarl on the other side. The handle rattled again and the door banged with increasing ferocity against the cabinet.

A one-inch gap appeared between the door and the jamb. It then disappeared and reappeared with alarming frequency. The frantic banging of wood crashing against metal filled the air and Gigi's head, making it hard to concentrate.

The apartment's isolation from the neighbours suddenly seemed a problem.

On his haunches, he pushed his back up against the cabinet, keeping the door shut. The small, sharp handles jabbed into Gigi's back and he wished he'd tipped it with the drawers facing the door. Too late now. He tilted his head, tensed his body, and swallowed the lump in his throat.

'Think, think, think,' he said to himself as the handles poked his tense body.

Surveying the room once more, he failed to see anything that might help him. There was no balcony, and jumping out of the window wasn't his preferred option. The mere thought of it made his head spin and his stomach do the same.

To distract himself from further discomfort, he turned his attention to the large en suite. Perhaps he imagined it, but a faint aroma of lavender wafted out through the open door and invited him in. A tranquil environment in which to barricade himself.

No, even if he could wait out the siege, then what? It would be like his wardrobe idea. Out of the frying pan and into prison. Running out of ideas, Gigi clasped his hands together, closed his eyes and whispered a quick prayer to the city's patron, St Maximus.

While he wouldn't call it a divine intervention, after exhaling his limbs merely tingled rather than shook and his lips parted slightly, but the movement lacked the conviction to form a smile. The saint might not have come down to earth and saved him, but he provided a plan. One that would not only see him escape, but with the document in hand.

***

Inside the van, Daniele rubbed his hands together, checked his watch, and then turned over the engine. It spluttered and coughed until, on the fourth try, it came alive.

The gentle humming of the machinery relaxed him while its heat rose through the bulkhead, giving the impression of a heated seat. He let both the engine and himself warm for a couple of minutes before putting the van into gear and heading down the Corso Galileo Ferraris, stopping only when he found a bar that was open.

He parked nearby, went in and ordered a coffee. There was time. After downing the florally scented liquid in one, he strode over to the public telephone in the far corner, all while cursing the weak acidic brew he'd just ingested.

After flicking the side of his nose with his thumb and sniffing, he leaned up against the wall, dropped a Gettone phone token into the machine, and, cradling the handset between his head and shoulder, dialled the only number he knew off by heart.

'Tell the boss it's Daniele. Yeah, I have a message from the janitor. The job is bigger than expected and he'll have to clean the whole house.'

Without waiting for a reply, Daniele hung up and returned to his vehicle.

He pulled out onto the road and swung left to join the opposite lane of traffic, heading to the roundabout on Corso Luigi Einaudi. Then he travelled for a few hundred yards before a rough gear change at yet another roundabout caused the van to screech in protest at its treatment. The turning had led him onto Corso Re Umberto, and in the opposite direction from where he'd just come.

The long-winded route enraged Daniele, and he alternated between cursing the one-way system and the van's spluttering old engine that threatened to betray him at any time. His tirade continued until he found himself outside the main gate of the prosecutor's building.

He stopped in the middle of the road and checked his watch. They were behind schedule. If the weasel faced *coglione* who'd ordered the job had given him the responsibility of the shooter, then none of this would have happened. Instead, the cuckold had laughed in his face, called him arrogant and told him to drive the 1,300-mile round trip. He'd made him a fucking chauffeur. At that memory, Daniele's large fingers squeezed the rim of the steering wheel, and his knuckles turned white as marble.

The jarring blare of a horn shook him from his fantasy of choking the capo. He checked the wing mirror to see a cream-coloured Fiat 500 with a woman's arm waving out from the side window.

'Bloody polenta eaters,' said Daniele, releasing one hand from the wheel to wave away the protest before pulling into a parking space a little further down by the corner of the building.

The compact car rumbled past and as it did, Daniele couldn't resist gesticulating his own thoughts to the woman who should have been home looking after the kids or cleaning, not out on her own clogging up the roads.

The van's engine remained idling as he calmed down and thought through his own options. Enzo had told him to be outside the gates, ready for a quick escape. He wondered if he should reverse down the street and get into the agreed position?

He scratched the back of his neck and wondered a little more. He could take the initiative and do it himself. And if the opportunity arose to take care of Enzo at the same time? Well, collateral damage *was* a part of the game. He smiled.

***

Shards of glass crunched beneath Enzo's heavy boots as he stepped away from the door. His jaw tightened and he snorted air out of his nose, resembling a bull about to charge. With his size, he was certain that he could break through the door and past whatever object stopped him from getting in.

His tongue ran over his front top teeth as he sized up the task. It wasn't the first time a job had turned complicated, but, like the professional he was, he would complete it by any means necessary.

The jarring blast of a car horn outside stole his attention, and in doing so, gave him the space to reassess the situation.

Sure, he could smash his way in and start firing. He had proven himself capable of detached brutality when required, but brute force had its limitations. It often created more problems than it solved.

Making the most of the opportunity, he closed his eyes, opened his mouth, and let the air flow in and out. It was this ability to step back and take a pragmatic approach to challenging situations that saw him rise and be successful. He'd do well to remember that. It was what marked him out from the more arrogant, hot-headed members of the organisation who would resort to ill-thought-out, rash and almost always violent action, costing them their lives either in a cell or in a box. He'd seen this happen to too many compatriots over the years, and, without guidance, he saw it happening to Daniele as well.

But it wasn't his future. There was more to him than the others. There had to be. Not just for his own survival, but for his family's prosperity.

The sense of perspective centred him, and he checked the time. He was further behind schedule. Daniele should be waiting outside right about now.

He tapped the barrel of the suppressor against his leg and considered his next move. When a situation was as strange as this one, it paid to be not only cautious, but curious.

He walked back down the hallway, and after placing the pistol down on the floor, he stood to the side of the window, located the cord, and raised the blinds slightly.

It took him a moment, and he needed to adjust his body to see out, but he spotted the van. The idiot hadn't followed instructions, but he would make it work. He returned the blinds to their lowered position.

After retrieving his weapon, he checked the other rooms. In the bedroom and bathroom, he flung open several cabinets and drawers and although he couldn't be certain, it looked like clothes and toiletries were missing. Another anomaly he wasn't expecting.

However, this revelation stirred up conflicting emotions in him. Despite his reservations, or rather fictional code, he had been prepared to eliminate the woman and child. Leaving any type of witness was bad for everyone. A witness didn't just turn you into a face for the police to hunt, but a liability for the clan. Every day, more and more penitents spoke up to relieve the burden on their souls and their jail terms. Trust was a hard thing to gain, and once you'd been implicated, it was impossible to keep. So their absence was a blessing.

He exhaled and allowed the tension to leave his body. The result was that his muscles, or perhaps his conscience, felt much lighter. Yet the shame of what he was prepared to do remained.

Everyone he'd ever killed played the game and knew the rules. Death hangs over us all. This acceptance helped him to bury the memories in a dark subconscious. However, on certain nights after too much alcohol, his mind replayed the last moments of his victims' lives. All twelve of them. Every time it happened as if it was a movie. When the first bullet entered their body, the camera would pan in on their pallid face. Then it would zoom in on their eyes, as the light faded into black. Although he would never admit it, especially not to himself, this sight made him feel powerful.

He scrunched his eyes and willed away the invasive waking dream. It was no good. His skin turned cold as the faces of his own wife and child appeared. Their flesh pale, as life drained from their eyes.

Beads of sweat had reformed on his brow and his head pounded as he shook it to shed the horrific images. A rhythmic whoosh of fast-flowing blood filled his ears, and a volcanic heat consumed his body. He gripped his pistol tight, ready to ram it into the head of the prosecutor for putting him in this situation. For dredging up what he had painstakingly hidden.

Then the pent-up anger erupted, creating a raging inferno that could only be extinguished in one way. And even though something seemed off with this whole situation, it no longer mattered. There was only one way to put out the fire, and that was to kill the man on the other side of the door.

But first, he had to get into that room.

***

As the rattling of the door subsided, Gigi considered his plan. What he was looking for could only be in one of three places. The filing cabinet blocking the door, a Venetian roll-top desk on the side wall, or the main work desk in front of him. The problem was, he only had time to check one. If that.

Within seconds, he assessed the probability and difficulty of each option. Despite having limited knowledge of the prosecutor's personality, he deduced that a man like that would possess an ordered, cautious, and professional nature. Even if his media performances were something that belonged on the televised variety show *L'Altra Domenica*.

Gigi ran his eyes over the neat desk and noticed the meticulously arranged stationery that rested before an empty document tray.

Two options remained.

The filing cabinet would be simple to pick, but it contained three large drawers, and he might have to go through at least two of them until he found what he wanted. That would take time. He was down to the last location.

His eyes turned to the walnut veneer roll-top desk, which gleamed even in this low light. Neoclassical in style, it must have cost as much as it weighed. But assuming it was genuine, and nobody had tampered with it, then the locks would be old and simple by today's standards.

Gigi's lips pressed together as his eyes narrowed and surveyed the three small drawers on the front and the larger cylinder on top. He visualised each lock, uncovering their weaknesses and secrets.

Then the door behind him shook with startling ferocity and gave him a start. He pounced forward to the ornate desk and quickly removed a shallow hook from his set of tools. His fingers moved with unrivalled dexterity as the lock yielded with little resistance.

Meanwhile, metal clanged and scraped as the momentum of the swaying filing cabinet saw it teetering one way before rocking back and crashing back against the door with a thud.

Gigi ignored it and remained focused the tambour of the desk rolled up and locked into the open position. He scanned the internal layout and considered the possibility of a hidden department. No, there was nothing secretive here. It would be in plain sight.

He licked his dry lips and scattered the files and folders laid out before him. His eyes moved across the writing on the covers and located the one he wanted before picking up the document and clutching it to his chest. As he did so, a warmth filled his body, and he became temporarily breathless. Stunned at his good fortune.

The frantic banging on the door fell into step with that of his own heart, but he had done it. Perhaps he wouldn't be killed after all. By this man or by whoever was behind Spaghettino hiring him. After all, you don't pay someone that much money to do a job like this and let them fail. Things had finally turned for him.

But there was no time for any positivity to take, and Gigi jumped as the cabinet crashed sideways onto the hard floor, causing a resounding clang to fill the air. His fingers tightened and scrunched the papers in his grip.

He froze on the spot as the door separated from the frame, transfixed as a beam of light grew millimetre by millimetre. Its insidious expansion seemed to defy time. But it also allowed Gigi the opportunity to work through the next step of his plan.

He rushed towards the window where he yanked the cord for the blinds, all but sending them flying up to the roof. He unclipped the small lock, swung the window open, and glanced out.

The sight caused a lump to catch in his throat as he considered. Could he do it?

'Let's cut a deal,' Gigi shouted over his shoulder. A final gambit, as much to avoid going through with his plan as it was to save his own skin and walk out the front door.

'Sure,' replied a deep, dispassionate voice. 'Come here and I'll kill you quickly.'

Gigi bit his lip and glanced out of the window one last time.

He swayed against the wall, tore off his left shoe and threw it out into the bright void. Then he kicked off the other shoe where he stood.

Now standing in his socks, he turned and glided across the smooth floor and into the toppled filing cabinet. He tossed the stolen document onto the desk where it landed with a slap, before shouting an unintelligible garble as he raised the cabinet up and back against both the ajar door and the fingers that had gained purchase along its edge.

A sickening crack sounded out, joined by a guttural scream as the door slammed closed.

The sound of pain and success propelled the adrenalin even faster around Gigi's body. Even so his head ached, and his mouth was dry. He couldn't think straight, but he didn't need to as his body had entered a primitive survival mode, relying on instinct and experience.

In one smooth motion, his legs thrust him forward, past the roll-top and the document, and into the adjacent en-suite bathroom. The constant banging of the door and the audible frustration of the intruder nipped at his heels.

The en suite was a medium-sized room. It contained a bidet, toilet, a cabinet, a large wicker basket for dirty clothing and a walk-in shower with a dark curtain pulled around it. Perfect for any workaholic to avoid having to see the family.

Gigi stared at the shower for a moment before chuckling to himself at the absurdity of his idea. Then, leaving the door open to suggest an empty room, he lifted the lid of the basket and clambered inside.

His body protested as he bent his knees up and squeezed himself in before becoming mummified in dirty laundry. But the clothes did little to muffle the thump of the cabinet as the office door finally opened.

***

Enzo's left shoulder throbbed as he barged forward into the gap. His broad shoulders momentarily wedged between the door and the frame before he could turn and slide through.

The tight squeeze caused him to stumble and trip over the corner of the fallen filing cabinet. He regained his balance, straightened up, and swept his pistol-holding right arm in an arc. The padding of his leather glove did little to ease the burning in his fingers as they gripped the gun. A reminder of the effort needed to get face-to-face with his adversary.

Now, having gained access, part of him wanted to blast away at everything. To relieve the tension that had built up in his skull. Mental wellbeing and relaxation tricks were all very well when things were going right, but in times of danger and stress you didn't need a hippy spouting crap, you just needed a gun.

Deep inside him, the old Enzo grew stronger. It was thanks to this darker side that he'd survived poverty and made something of his life. Unlike his father, who kept his morals but lost the family home and plunged them all into life on the streets. That wasn't Enzo's future, though. He would do whatever it took to provide for his kids. He was the better man.

A light breeze drifted in from the open window and cooled his skin. He turned towards it and noticed the lone shoe on the floor. It wasn't possible that the target had escaped, was it?

He stormed across to the window, positioned himself to the left, and glanced out. Then he moved to the other side and repeated the action.

There it was. The second shoe.

He leaned back onto the wall and exhaled before crouching down, placing the gun beside him and taking off his gloves.

For a minute he shook out his tender fingers and considered what could have happened. From this part of the building, if the man had jumped, it was likely that Daniele wouldn't have seen him, and even if that idiot saw a guy with no shoes hobbling down the street, he wouldn't have thought to stop him.

One word summed this situation up. Fucked.

Ever the pragmatist, Enzo did what had kept him alive all these years. He accepted the position he was in and moved forward with a new plan.

His instructions were explicit. To kill the prosecutor. Yes, but why? To postpone the investigation until a more amenable prosecutor was assigned. That was the crux of the issue. That was what he needed to do. His dark eyes narrowed and surveyed the space, looking for something that could help him achieve his goal. And keep him alive.

The problem was, he didn't know what he was looking for. It was then he noticed the second door.

He put his gloves back on and lifted his weapon. As the barrel of the suppressor tapped against his right thigh, more thoughts filled Enzo's head.

With a sigh, he strolled towards the en suite, paused on the threshold, and looked inside. His brow furrowed at this unexpected room.

As he stood, embracing the light aroma of lavender, an almost imperceptible breeze rolled in from the office window and caused the navy shower curtain to ripple.

He smirked at the movement. *Surely not?* The thought of such a childish hiding place made him tut and shake his head. He'd have had some respect had the man jumped out of the window.

Still, he was a professional and knew better than to be complacent. His face hardened as he raised the pistol to head height.

Double tap.

The bullets tore through the fabric before a sharp crack preceded an avalanche of porcelain as fragments of tiles crashed to the ground.

Enzo's forehead creased at the unexpected sound. He marched over and yanked the torn curtain down, revealing a shower area filled with pieces of tile but no body.

His eyes settled on the battered wall. The bullets had embedded themselves deep. *Shit*. He would need to dump the weapon before heading back. That also meant there was no need to worry about picking up the ejected cartridges either. This job had turned messier.

The distant blaring of a horn stole his attention away from the detritus and he glanced over his shoulder in its direction.

Less than a minute later, he was at the balcony door, once again angling his body to look down on the street.

There was no further sound, and no vehicles occupied the road. Perhaps it had just been a driver blocking the street? It didn't matter. He had a job to finish.

***

Gigi waited sixty seconds from when the assassin left the room and then waited a little longer. The inside of his cheek burned from where he'd chewed it in order to control his fear and, more importantly, his movement. He knew it wouldn't take much to topple over in this casket of dirty clothes.

By now, he figured the man must have been gone for a couple of minutes, and the obnoxious sound of a horn outside had long since stopped. Whatever had caused it, he hoped it scared the thug off.

Still unwilling to risk it all, Gigi raised his head until his eyes peeped over the rim of the basket. The wicker lid wobbled on his hair.

Clear.

Moisture formed around the corner of his eyes, and without thinking, he grabbed a cotton sock and dabbed it away. The smell made his head tilt back, and his nostrils flare and twitch. There was little he could control as his eyes scrunched and his chest expanded.

He buried his face in a mass of clothing, which absorbed the sound and the mucus.

After rubbing his nose, he clambered out of the basket and returned to the office.

The low murmuring of vehicles filtered through the open window along with the frigid morning breeze, which caused Gigi to shiver.

As he headed to the roll-top desk, his attention flittered between his prize and the open door that led to the hallway.

The only sound came from the infrequent traffic outside, and so he risked it.

Standing over the antique desk, he picked up the folder and flicked through it, scanning the names of those indicted. He was surprised at how many he recognised. These were people who were always in the papers for all the right reasons. People above suspicion.

He cleared his throat, stifling the sound as much as he could manage, before continuing to glance through the pages. When he reached the details about the charges, he dropped the document back on the desk and looked away.

Politicians and organised-crime bosses had always mingled. It was how permits got passed and the economy worked. Most people accepted this reality and as long as the honest workers received their pay, there wasn't a problem. It was just the way things were.

Sure, the growing industrial cities of the north didn't require the copious numbers of concrete apartment blocks that sprung up on the outskirts, especially when they were built without supporting infrastructure, and those southern motorways that never quite took the direct route to their destination existed solely to extend the budgets and coffers of the gangs in charge. But those were business decisions. This was simply wicked.

Corruption, terror and violence had become commonplace in Italian society. And like all crimes, they left victims. Those who remained behind had to get on with things, while those who were gone no longer had to worry. But victims of human trafficking had to just exist. Endure. And Gigi didn't know how he could live with himself if he allowed anyone to suffer from being reduced to a nameless commodity.

Gigi rubbed his chin while considering what to do next. If he failed to provide these documents, then whoever bankrolled Spaghettino would kill him. What good was being virtuous if you were dead?

Lost in the conundrum, it took him a few extra seconds to connect the return of the bleating car horn, the crashing of a table, and the thud of approaching footsteps.

He just made it to the doorway in time to see the imposing figure storming down the hallway towards him.

The sight caused Gigi's jaw to drop, and a high-pitched squeal to fly out of his mouth.

His heart pounded and limbs trembled as he jerked back, slammed the door shut and hauled up the filing cabinet to slow down his attacker's entry.

As Gigi's legs wobbled more and more with each bang of the door, his breath became shallow, and it took everything he had to speak.

'Do you want the prosecutor or the document?'

The banging stopped.

***

Daniele's fingers tapped furiously against the thin plastic steering wheel, building in intensity until his palms hammered the instrument, pounding it like a drum.

He had little to do but observe his surroundings, and from his parking spot he'd noticed the same Giulietta go past three times. Given the long-winded one-way system, even taking a wrong turn shouldn't have seen it come back that many times.

To make matters worse, a dark blue Alfa Romeo Giulia appeared to have joined it. However, on its second time around, that vehicle continued across the intersection instead of turning left down Via Governolo and parked up only a few hundred metres away from him.

They were too far away for Daniele to see who the passengers were, but he had a pretty good idea. He wasn't stupid after all, and he didn't believe in coincidence.

He finished his drum solo with an emphatic smash of the horn before winding down the window, leaning out, and checking the Giulia for movement.

The front passenger door of the suspicious vehicle opened, a head appeared momentarily, and then disappeared back into the car.

Daniele took a quick breath before smiling at his cleverness. They had waited too long and been rumbled. To Daniele, this confirmed his suspicions that Enzo wasn't up to the job. That man over-thought things. He was too slow. Too ancient. Just like the bosses.

The old guys needed to move aside. They spent too much time sitting around playing *scopa* and talking. If the clan was to prosper, it required men of action to take charge. Men like him. He didn't need to wait for ages thinking things through. To him, the right idea came quickly, and he had the balls to act on it. He was decisive. A leader. And now, with the fuzz closing in, he needed to make another decision.

Daniele figured that the second vehicle was circling back round, ready to box him in. A typical police manoeuvre. One he was too smart to fall for.

His eyes scanned as much of the surrounding area as they could, darting towards every available mirror. There was no sense in both he and Enzo getting pinched.

With a rapid movement, his arms flew off the wheel, one hand turned the key in the ignition, and the other jerked the gearstick into reverse. Then his foot stomped on the pedal, the tyres squealed, a plume of black smoke fired out of the exhaust, and the van rocketed back and into the middle of the street.

The foul stench of petrol permeated inside the vehicle, but, undeterred, Daniele shoved the gearstick into first and then second, building up speed before taking a hard left. As he drove, he jabbed the horn. It was the only warning he could give Enzo, and more than that man deserved.

As the van raced down the street, Daniele's head felt heavy. The fumes had filled his nostrils, and the blaring of the horn still rattled around inside his skull, but he ignored the discomfort and pushed the pedal to the floor. Within a minute, the speedometer matched his heartbeat.

Less than thirty seconds later, a siren wailed behind him.

He glanced in the rear-view mirror and saw the enemy advancing. The van felt as if it was burning up, but that might have been his skin. The surrounding cars parked along the street disappeared in a blur. He'd nearly made it to the intersection. A laugh scraped its way out of his dry throat as the possibility of escape grew ever larger.

Consumed by hope, he leaned forward in his seat and willed the van to gain an extra few kilometres an hour.

The chasing siren stopped, and Daniele checked his mirror again, but as he stared in confusion at the now-static police car, he didn't notice the Giulietta that blocked the bottom of the street.

He felt the impact of the windshield against his head before he could understand what had happened. The car twisted sideways as his body flew out in a hail of glass.

The world spun.

He landed with a sickening thud on the roof of the Alfa.

***

Gigi's right foot tapped the floor for what seemed an eternity as he waited for a response from his assailant.

Instead, the screeching of tyres, sirens, and the incessant beep of a horn from outside punctured the silence shared between the two men. It was too much for Gigi to take. His clammy hands were itchy under his thin gloves, and he felt jittery. He sniffed at his shoulder and was repelled by the odour that clung to him.

'I'm not the man you want, so let's strike a deal and both get out of here. OK?' said Gigi.

'You're in the prosecutor's apartment, eating his food. What makes you think you aren't the man I want?'

Gigi racked his brain for the right answer. Every probable outcome was like a blow to the head. If this man came here to kill the prosecutor, he wouldn't hesitate to kill a nobody.

'Listen to my deal,' Gigi said with the speed of a machine gun and as much confidence as he could muster. His voice shifted an octave of its own accord.

'What can you offer me that I won't get by killing you?'

The response sent a chill down Gigi's spine. Or perhaps that was because of the breeze coming through the window. He wondered whether the option to jump was still there. If he was lucky, he'd only suffer a sprained ankle and then he could run to safety. Well, hobble. With what he'd learned, if he did hand over the documents, maybe his employers would sort him out with some medical care. Or having served his purpose, would they treat him like a lame horse and put him down?

'Time,' said Gigi, surprising even himself as he paced the room.

'Go on,' said the man. 'Although it's running out for both of us.'

'Exactly. I'm in here and you're out there. You'd have to get to me before the pigs come and get you. But if we make an agreement, we can both be on our way. Free men. Do you want to hear my proposal?'

***

Enzo nodded as he listened to the guy barricaded in the office. He had to concede that nobody had the time for a siege. Therefore, the more the man talked, the more it made sense. Not only that, while one Northern accent was as guttural as the next, this man didn't sound like a well-educated prosecutor. Not even an assistant. Perhaps he was an innocent workman, after all.

At that moment, Enzo looked down at his still throbbing right hand. His face set to stone and his body tensed. While the act of killing him wouldn't satisfy his boss, it would make him feel better.

With his left hand, Enzo pinched the bridge of his nose and scrunched up his eyes.

'OK, shut up and listen. This is the plan. Open the door and pass the documents through.'

'I'm not opening it.'

'Fine. Slide them under the door, and I'll be on my way.'

'And you won't wait for me outside?'

'Neither of us has the time to finish this business. Besides, I don't know who you are, and you don't know me,' said Enzo as an idea formed in his head, and made his lips curl up into a smile.

***

Gigi slumped down, his back pressed up against the filing cabinet. He sighed as the tension faded and his muscles weakened, leaving him drained him of energy.

The man on the other side of the door had proposed a solid plan. More than that, there appeared to be no other way to get out alive. Although it might mean death afterwards. Perhaps he would take a trip away somewhere. Use the advance he'd received to enjoy what little of life remained.

He covered his head in his trembling hands. Whether it lasted a moment or a minute, Gigi couldn't say. He'd barely considered his response before an agitated voice demanded one.

'OK, let me see how I can do this.'

He pressed his palms down onto the ground, pushed himself up, and stared at the hefty folder. It was too big to fit under the door in its entirety. Maybe he could just give the guy some of the crap and keep the rest. The best of both worlds. Survival against both sets of thugs.

A shaky laugh rattled out through his parted mouth, as he decided the idiot wouldn't know the difference. Besides, there was no time for him to look at what he'd received. Nor would he understand. After all, the man was a killer, not a to-order thief.

The thought caused Gigi to pause. He had no reason to trust the man. While there was still honour among thieves, that didn't extend to violent mercenaries who only cared for money. No, once the brute had got what he wanted, subtlety and Gigi would be redundant. Regardless of what he promised, no professional would leave a witness.

'Give me a minute,' said Gigi as he scanned the main office desk, spotting what he needed.

He reached the desk in four strides and grabbed a long steel ruler before returning to the cabinet.

'I'm going to move the filing cabinet to the side so I can slide the documents under the door. There are –' Gigi counted at least fifty pages – 'twenty pages here. If you try anything, I'll slam the cabinet back in place and scream for the police out of the window.'

After the man grunted his agreement, Gigi slid the cabinet aside, causing it to groan in protest at its latest mistreatment. Leaving a corner of it blocking the handle, he withdrew the first and last ten pages from the folder.

He moved to the opposite side of the door, crouched down, and used the ruler to slide the sheets of paper beneath the door, two at a time. His position keeping him out of the way of the door.

Every time a couple of inches of paper disappeared to the other side, the rest of the sheet would be yanked through with the enthusiasm of a child offered a *gianduja* chocolate. The image lightened the mood and gave him the strength to keep going.

After pushing the seventeenth and eighteenth pieces, he noted a slight noise on the other side of the door. The sound of death was almost a relief. It proved his senses were still with him.

His eyes darted across the gap towards the filing cabinet and the door handle, and back down to the final two sheets of paper.

He swallowed hard and used the ruler to push the last pieces of paper under the door and over the threshold. His body trembled and he had to fight to keep his balance and positioning.

The white sheets began their slow journey. An inch. Two. Three.

Gigi's head pounded. *Why hadn't the man taken them yet? When was he going to make his move?*

Three holes exploded in the door at stomach height. Wood splintered.

Still positioned at the side of the door, Gigi rose and using the last of his strength pulled down the filing cabinet, extinguishing the beams of light that filtered through the circular gaps in the door.

Three more bullets tore through the door, higher this time, sending shards of wood across Gigi's hair and face.

Then the room blurred, as a cacophony of sounds swirled all around him.

***

Enzo bent down and, after placing the warm pistol on the floor, checked his boss's name was on the documents. The last thing he wanted to do was to go through all of this only to return with scrap.

Once he was satisfied he had what was needed, he folded the sheets and shoved them into his waistband.

He grabbed his gun, straightened up and went to confirm his kill, but his hand hovered over the handle, held in place by the growing whine of sirens.

The noise seemed to circle the building like a shiver of sharks, and Enzo knew he would have to shoot his way to the van.

His stiff fingers tightened around the metal. His head snapped to the side and his eyes widened as the entrance door exploded inwards with a deafening crash. Its hinges squealed in protest, barely clinging to the splintering frame.

Two stocky Carabinieri officers stepped through into the hallway, one in front and one behind to the left, their Beretta M12 submachine guns raised and ready.

Enzo gritted his teeth as desperation, hatred and contempt consumed him. The bastards standing before him were just more cogs in a machine that had subjugated the south. Profiting from his fellow *Calabresi* while denying them their share of Italy's economic boom.

He swung his pistol up, slid his index finger towards the trigger, and roared like a Calabrian lion.

The first bullet sent a wave of heat across his chest as air burst out of his lungs and mouth. His body jerked at the impact. Several more slugs penetrated his flesh and launched him backwards.

As he crashed down, the back of his skull bounced off the hard floor. An image of his wife and child flashed behind his eyes. They stared back at him. Cold. Ashamed. Abandoned.

His vision blurred, while a bell rattled inside his head. The shrill noise bounced from ear to ear. A small drop of blood seeped from the side of his mouth as his body numbed.

As the final pieces of lead punctured his skin, a faint metallic scent swept over him. Then the lights turned off.

***

Gigi's legs wobbled as he stumbled across the spinning room and into the bathroom. The unmistakable roar of gunfire made his hair stand on end, and he was thankful to reach his comforting sanctuary of wicker.

Ensconced inside, he wrapped a creased pair of slacks around his head and scrunched his eyes closed. He embraced the near silence that followed.

Then the sound of laughter filled the now-disconcerting void.

As the merriment grew, Gigi freed himself from the restrictive trousers and moved his face up against the coarse wicker and squinted through a narrow gap.

His stomach tensed as the dark blue uniform of a Carabinieri came into view and made Gigi gasp. His jaw crunched down hard and veins popped to the fore of his neck and forehead as he stifled any further noise. In return for this exertion, his lungs ached.

Yet he endured because someone had come to his rescue. In a manner of speaking, at least.

The deep footsteps of the officer echoed like thunder on the exposed wood floor, and as the man approached the bathroom door, Gigi saw the shiny black semi-automatic that dangled at his waist.

'Clear,' said the man. 'Just some holes in the shower. We'll call it in.' He turned and strolled through the office and out into the hall.

Gigi's puffed-out cheeks deflated, and he exhaled. The experience proved a great relief, but as his breathing returned to normal, he inhaled the odour of his own dry sweat alongside several days' worth of used clothing.

'So, who was the guy shooting at before us?' said a distant voice.

'Who knows, but it looks like he got away. Put out a call looking for a man with no shoes,' said the second officer with a laugh. The same hearty chuckle as he'd heard before.

The officers remained for a couple more minutes before the slamming of the front door told Gigi he was safe. He clambered out of the basket and stretched out. A dull ache ran along his spine, and he groaned.

He entered the office, retrieved the documents he'd left on the desk, and then, holding back the nausea, took the bloodstained ones still tucked into the waistband of the would-be assassin. The poor man reminded him of a pincushion. He stared down at the corpse and made the sign of the cross. You can't grieve forever, though, especially not for someone who tried to kill you, so, with the time for sympathy over, Gigi rolled up the combined sheets of paper and headed into the master bedroom.

The room, like all the others, was meticulously well-organised and easy to navigate. Gigi pulled open the double doors of the mahogany wardrobe and perused the items. He lifted the hangers and held the clothing up against himself as if he was in a shop.

In under five minutes, he'd dressed himself in an ill-fitting suit and squeezed his feet into a pair of English loafers. He returned to the kitchen, shoved his old clothes into a large bin, and sighed at the food that still covered the table and floor. *Leave no trace*. The thought of tidying up did appeal to him, but the Carabinieri had already been in and noted the state of the place. Why complicate matters?

Hungrier than ever, he headed to the front door and peered out of the peephole into the dark and empty communal area. He gripped the handle and pushed it down at half-speed. His hand shook at the control needed to remain calm.

He sighed in relief as the latch clicked and the door opened. But he wasn't safe yet. He poked his head out of the door and listened. Nothing. His eyes clocked the ancient single-door lift that occupied the space halfway down the corridor. Its uninviting metal gate proved too uninviting. The last thing he needed was to be stuck in there. So, he walked along the corridor and descended the wide spiral stairs.

Two Carabinieri officers, he presumed the same ones from earlier, waited at the bottom. At the sight of their right hands hovering over their weapons, Gigi fought to keep his legs from collapsing under him. He glanced at their faces, doing his best to avoid direct eye contact. Their eyes appeared black and their faces hard as stone. He could sense them staring at him as he shuffled down the stairs and into the lobby. Beneath his clothing, his skin turned cold and his stomach twisted in knots.

As he came level with them, the shortest of the two held up a hand and looked Gigi up and down.

'Name, apartment, and identity card, sir.'

By now, Gigi's body felt like jelly, and his voice wavered before he caught himself and cleared his throat.

'Cossiga. Third floor. I didn't think I needed identification to go for a stroll?'

The shorter officer's gaze ran over Gigi's loose clothing and unkempt hair.

Gigi sensed the distrust and knew he had to act fast.

'As I said, I'm Professor Cossiga. Third floor. Do I need to return to get my identity? Perhaps, at the same time, I'll call your superiors and tell them of your ignorance?'

With a sigh, the officer tilted his head and allowed Gigi on his way.

As he approached the exit, the taller officer rushed over, pulled the door open and wished the *professore* a good day.

By now, the morning clouds had dissipated and the wind died down. Gigi strolled past the gaggles of reporters and emergency workers without attracting a second glance.

He turned right onto Corso Luigi Einaudi and kept to the shadows that hugged the imposing building, stopping only once to stare at a lonely shoe on the ground.

The sight reminded him he was only halfway out of this situation. He patted the documents in his pocket and wondered what to do next.

As his mind and his feet wandered in different directions, he found himself outside the large glass window of a *pasticceria*. His eyes widened at the heavenly vision of freshly baked pastries of all shapes, sizes, and flavours, and he could not help but lick his lips. The next thing he knew, he was inside, standing next to the pastry counter.

From cocoa and cinnamon to orange and pistachio, his nose inhaled the tantalising aromas, while a small drop of drool fell from the corner of his mouth.

He ordered a hazelnut croissant along with a bicerin, the traditional drink of the city comprising an espresso layered with chocolate and cream, and sat down at a nearby table. It cost a little more, but considering the events of that morning, he deserved something extra.

The stolen documents poked into his ribs, and with some reluctance, Gigi pulled them out from under his clothing and placed them face down on the table next to his drink and snack.

He pursed his lips and looked around. The neighbouring tables were empty save for a copy of that day's edition of local newspaper *La Stampa*. He grabbed it and slammed it on top of his bounty. Then he took a bite of the croissant and, as the sugar rush hit him, so did an idea.

He shot up off the chair, his knees bashing the underside of the table, spilling his drink over the newspaper. But he didn't notice as he rushed to the telephone and shoved in a token.

'*Ciao*, Dario. Are you working today? Perfect, I have something for you. I'll be there in thirty minutes.'

The arrangement finalised, Gigi scoffed down the last of his breakfast and called Spaghettino to confirm the exchange.

But first he had an appointment with his friend over at the newspaper. Those responsible might evade justice, but exposure? Not while Gigi took breath.

Dance of Suspicion

Gigi stepped off the train and paused on Platform 4 of Milano Centrale station. As one hand gripped his briefcase, the other patted his pockets as he went through the ritual of checking that he had everything.

This was his first visit to the city, and before he could even comprehend the height of the arched train shed or absorb the strange combination of odours that exist in a place of human transience, a plump man, whose waist was being strangled in a slim-fit suit, disembarked from the train and barged into Gigi.

Gigi's eyes widened as he flew forward, mouth open, and crashed into an attractive woman who was craning her neck to see along the platform.

He offered his best smile and apologised. She swore at him and stormed off.

Meanwhile, the fat man had already waddled a hundred yards towards the exit, oblivious.

With a sigh, Gigi dropped his case to the ground and passed a smoothing hand down the front of his inconspicuous yet itchy woollen suit.

Satisfied at his appearance, he picked up his briefcase, which certainly made carrying his tools a lot easier, and weaved his way between the bodies of frustrated commuters flocking towards the exit for the metropolis.

As he moved, the thick, coarse fabric of the suit's collar chafed the back of his neck and reminded him of why he only dressed up for court. Without breaking stride, and not wanting to be late, Gigi turned his head side to side in a desperate act to ease the irritation, but succeeded only in attracting the attention of those around him.

While he'd taken every effort to blend in, to be anonymous, he refused to suffer for his art, and he was thankful the glances were fleeting. All except one.

The man had a large moustache and wore a navy peacoat. As Gigi got closer, the guy stepped forward and raised a palm.

'Easy, *Mandrino*,' said the man with a crooked smile, before introducing himself as Inspector Sacchetti of the state police.

Gigi's muscles tensed – in stark contrast to his heart, which hammered away. This was a first. Busted before even starting the job.

'Don't worry,' said the inspector, as he peered over Gigi's shoulder and then checked the surrounding area. 'There are a lot of pickpockets operating around here, so I'm just making some routine checks to ensure passengers are safe. Can I see your identification?'

As he spoke, the inspector's knee trembled, causing Gigi to glance down at the movement and confirm his initial thoughts. No inspector would be on duty wearing bell bottoms.

Unwilling to cause a scene - as it wouldn't do either of them any good - Gigi played along. With an exaggerated sigh, he placed his briefcase on the floor in front of him and then dug a hand into his inside jacket pocket. His fingers flicked between several cards, a skill he'd practised over recent months, before withdrawing a fake identity card.

He offered it to the inspector.

As the smooth hands of the state official reached out, Gigi pulled the card back. 'Could I see *your* identification first, Inspector?'

The two men locked eyes. The bustling crowd around them blurred into the background, while the voice on the PA system faded into a monotonous drone.

Gigi noted the man's hands had dropped to his sides, fists clenched, while his Adam's apple bobbed up and down.

'Look, Inspector, I don't mean to offend you, but you never know who you're talking to,' said Gigi with a half smile.

The Inspector's face scrunched up, and Gigi knew he had him. It took all his self-control to keep his own facial muscles impassive as a grin threatened to break out.

After savouring the moment, Gigi gave in and smiled. 'You're right. Sorry, here's my details,' he said, stepping forward.

His foot knocked into the briefcase, and he toppled over and into the inspector.

With no semblance of grace, Gigi grabbed his unwilling partner and led him through an awkward tango. Their limbs flayed while fingers clawed into anything that would help the men recover their balance.

The dance lasted as long as Gigi needed it to. When he was ready, he planted a foot on the ground and relaxed his muscles to absorb the movement of his unsuspecting victim.

By the end of the uncomfortable embrace, Gigi had observed no gun on the inspector's body, but a fat wallet instead.

Now disentangled, the men stepped away from each other, and Gigi spotted two Carabinieri officers milling about at the bottom of the platform. 'Your lot?' he asked, raising his chin in their direction.

The inspector pivoted to see who Gigi was talking about. By the time he turned back, his face had drained of colour. The effect made his deep-set eyes appear almost cadaverous.

'Just move on,' said the inspector. His body twitched and he glanced around the platform, before settling his gaze on a departing train.

Taking his cue, Gigi retrieved his case and proffered another apology as he walked away, keeping his steps even until he'd passed the officers.

Safe beyond their view, he raced through the grand Arrivals Hall, ignoring the aroma of freshly ground coffee that wafted from the cafes and the acrid stench of cigarettes from the men standing chatting at the newsstands.

He headed left, disappearing momentarily behind the colonnades before emerging outside. Beneath the small clock, he met Matteo.

The acquaintances nodded to each other and made their way in silence towards a dark Fiat 126.

With Gigi slumped in the passenger seat, the vehicle crawled along the Via Tonale, as Milan's commuters stifled the flow of traffic. Not that Gigi noticed. Instead, he fixed his attention on the contents of the so-called inspector's wallet. Besides a few cards, there were over three thousand lire tucked inside. His lips curled into a wry grin. Not bad for a couple of minutes' work.

Matteo nodded at the wad of notes in Gigi's lap. 'Petrol ain't cheap, you know.'

Luck Be a Lady

Gigi grinned as he pressed down on the horn of the Alfa Romeo. He had never driven a Giulia before, let alone the latest model, but so far that appeared to be the only perk of his new job as a chauffeur.

As the abrasive sound died in the still night air, he turned off the engine and got out. He stared at the imposing countryside villa in front of him, rolled his palms down the front of his creased white shirt and straightened his tie.

He'd spent the night driving the pretentious, narcissistic assholes of Torino, and sighed at the thought of one more rich prick to endure. Still, it was better than spending fifty hours a week getting steam in his face and slinging coffees across a bar. And his criminal record certainly limited his work opportunities.

That said, this last fare was an airport drop-off that required him to drive forty minutes east to the town of Chivasso before taking the client north to the airport itself, and then heading home. All in, it was over ninety minutes of driving, and thirty minutes more than he was being paid for.

Still, his colleagues back at the depot told him these jobs often resulted in a good tip. They said something about people being excited about travelling abroad. He wouldn't know. The only time he ever went away it was at the state's expense.

Shaking his head, Gigi kicked a square pebble across the gravel driveway and approached the stone steps that led to the main door. Out of the corner of his eye, he saw a Ferrari convertible and smiled. He paused on the first step and turned to get a better look.

'Driver! What are you waiting for? Come up here now and get my luggage!'

The gruff voice snapped Gigi back to reality. It was show time. He nodded at the portly gentleman in a suit who stood in the open doorway and ran up the steps. 'I'm so sorry, sir. Leave your bags for me.' He knew that the more he grovelled, the bigger the tip would be.

'Of course I'll bloody leave them for you,' said the client before running his eyes up and down Gigi's attire. 'Come on, check-in opens in an hour. Quick! What are you doing? Stop. Clean your shoes first. This rug cost more than you earn in a week.'

After rubbing his heels against a spotless mat, Gigi entered the house. 'This is a beautiful home,' he said as his eyes darted from side to side, appraising the art deco vase on the mahogany hallway table, the Mannerist painting on the wall, and the lack of any items belonging to a wife or kids.

'Yes, and I earned it. If you worked harder, you might have achieved something like this,' said the client.

'Yeah,' said Gigi as an image of his dark and dirty apartment flashed through his mind. The thought depressed him, and he decided he'd visit a bar on the way home to lift his spirits. Or at least top them up to stop them dropping even lower.

'The bags are still all there, waiting for you,' said the client, nodding towards the luggage.

Gigi looked down at a large duffel bag, two suitcases, and a small briefcase. He swung the strap of the bag over one shoulder and, with a grunt, lifted the suitcases, knocking down the briefcase, before heading to the car. 'Follow me, sir.'

He stumbled forward, the oversized canvas bag too heavy for his sloped shoulders. It slid down and crashed against the floor. Gigi abandoned the bag to a series of curses from the client and promised to rush back to get it.

The two suitcases landed in the boot of the Alfa with a deep thud, followed by an exasperated sigh from the client who stood watching him. Gigi half smiled at the man, before rushing round the side and opening the right rear passenger door. The client got into the vehicle without a word. Just a long look at his watch once he'd sat down.

'I'll just go back for the rest of your items, sir.' It was obvious he hadn't given a good impression so far, but there was still time to improve the value of the tip.

The client sighed again, and with exaggerated effort, reached into his pocket and withdrew a keyring with several keys. 'Wait, lock up afterwards. It's the black-and-white tipped one. You are capable of that, aren't you?'

Gigi snatched the key, and whether it was his shoes turning in the gravel or his teeth grinding together, his only reply was a low scraping sound.

A voice chased him into the villa, telling him to be quick about it.

He grabbed the duffel bag and took a moment to glance into some of the other rooms. A 25-inch TV. A Technics turntable. Glassware from Murano. How the other half live. Gigi's jaw tightened and, as he turned, his right shoe bumped against something.

His eyes dropped and focused on the leather briefcase. And at how a distortion of his own dishevelled appearance was reflected in its gleaming buckles. Gigi frowned before booting it under the hallway table. He smiled, satisfied at his petty act of defiance.

The blare of a car horn caused Gigi to freeze. It sounded again, snapping him back into action as he hoisted the duffel bag onto his shoulder and rushed outside. Through narrowed eyes, he saw the client leaning between the front seats and smacking the steering wheel.

He flicked through the keys, noting the Ferrari logo before selecting the one in the colours of Juventus. He locked up and raced back to the back of the car, where he threw the bag into the boot and slammed it shut before flinging himself into the front seat, where the overpowering stench of the client's cologne filled his nostrils and caused him to sneeze onto the dashboard.

After wiping it clean with his sleeve, he checked the rear-view mirror. The client was staring, tight-faced, straight ahead. Gigi gulped, shoved the gearstick into first and the vehicle, with a loud growl, sped off down the driveway, leaving a trail of dust in its wake.

As they merged onto the busy motorway, the hum of the engine and the rush of wind through the open windows filled the car and lightened Gigi's mood. So much so that he was even willing to give the client another chance.

With one eye glued to the speedometer, he attempted some small talk, only to be cut off with a terse reply every time. The client had, however, divulged that he was going abroad for a business meeting. The importance of which would undoubtedly be over Gigi's head. At that point, the two men settled into an uncomfortable silence, broken only by the occasional cough from the client, which was always followed by an exaggerated checking of his watch.

***

'Here we are, sir, Torino airport. I went as fast as I could, so you still have thirty minutes to check in,' said Gigi, looking over his shoulder.

'Yes, you could have killed me going at that speed. Your boss will hear about this.'

Before Gigi could respond, a spirited porter yanked open the passenger door.

'Get my bags off the driver and send them to my plane for Frankfurt,' said the client, before striding through the sliding doors and into the check-in area.

The cheap bastard couldn't even spare enough change for a coffee. Gigi stepped out of the car and walked round to the back, where he hauled out the three pieces of luggage. He slammed the boot down with a crash and turned to see the porter standing there, palm out and nodding towards the bags.

Gigi shrugged. 'Cigarette?'

The porter gave a sympathetic smile and nodded. Gigi shoved a hand into his rumpled trousers. As he grabbed the crumpled pack, his fingers felt something metallic. His brow furrowed, and along with the cigarettes he withdrew a small set of keys.

He offered the pack to the beleaguered worker, who took one cigarette and returned the rest. As the porter loaded the bags onto a rickety steel trolley, Gigi put the pack away and turned the keys over in his hand.

A few seconds passed before opportunity hit him in the face, causing his eyes to widen. He jumped back into the Alfa with a smile that beamed brighter than the car's headlights.

***

The Giulia gobbled up the tarmac of the *autostrada Torino* as if it hadn't had a meal for weeks. In just over twenty minutes Gigi arrived at the Orco river, which marked the boundary of Chivasso.

As the signs for the centre appeared, he checked the dashboard clock and decided there was time for a detour. The villa would be his all night, but the bars would only be open for another hour at the most.

Gigi hit the indicator to signal right and headed towards the centre, where he parked up just past the octagonal tower. He glanced at the structure, once part of a grand castle but now surrounded by small shops and apartments. He shrugged as he got out of the car and strolled into the bustling Piazza della Repubblica.

Revellers laughed, jeered, and drank the night away, their joy illuminated by the tall street lamps that ran the length of the rectangular piazza. The intoxicating aroma of alcohol, food and expensive perfumes flooded the space, and Gigi briefly experienced the beautiful life, if only in his head.

The thought of finding a table and making that dream a reality, however, never crossed his mind. These weren't his kind of people. And he wasn't their type, either. What value was there in discussing which political party was in power, or how the economy was doing? Those things never improved his life. No, he was content to just shoot some pool and have a beer.

His feet continued to pound the cobbles and directed him towards the collegiate church of Santa Maria Assunta. The high-pitched squeals of laughter faded into the background. He turned left just before reaching the holy building and pushed open a splintered wooden door on which hung a wooden sign saying 'Bar'.

Inside, stale cigarette smoke mixed with the pungent odour of stale alcohol and caused his eyes to water. He pushed his way through the oppressive fug and towards the counter, where he sat down on a stool and ordered a beer.

After taking a swig, Gigi swung around and surveyed his fellow patrons. Shadows and silhouettes populated the far corners, their features masked by the smoke. Despite this, in the mirror behind the bar he could still make out the usual losers that you would expect to see in a place like this. They were everyday people. Like him.

He continued to case the joint, hoping to find a companion for the night. There were always a few women in a place like this, although they sometimes proved to be more hassle than they were worth. But it had been more than a few months since Gigi experienced the pleasure of that type of trouble.

The alcohol was going down easily now, and with increased confidence his gaze settled on two women who sat at a central table. They stood out from everyone else. It wasn't just their style, but their auras, too. Not that Gigi believed in such nonsense. He noticed that next to their glasses of white wine was a pristine Italian phrase book. Foreigners.

With enormous eyes, Gigi admired the women's beautiful necklaces, worth a few thousand lire each, and shiny earrings which he valued at about the same.

He fanned out his collar and rotated his shoulders. As he hopped off his seat, he felt like a lion about to pounce on its prey. He swaggered over to the table, coughed, and when the two angels looked up, asked if he could sit down. Before they could refuse, he'd placed himself between them and jabbed at the language guide.

'Would you ladies care for a guided tour of our beautiful town?'

'It's OK, thank you. We're leaving tomorrow for Torino,' said the plump, dark-haired woman on the right.

'But we always have tonight,' said Gigi, wondering where that smooth line came from. He widened his smile, plying them with what he hoped they'd take for typical Italian charm.

With a curious look towards Gigi and then each other, the two women each took a sip of their wine, their eyes meeting in silent agreement.

'I have a beautiful villa on the outskirts of town. We could continue our drinks there and then tomorrow morning, before you leave, I'll drive you to all the sights.' He blurted out his offer, loud enough for all those around him to hear.

The women exchanged a knowing glance once again. The plump brunette pursed her lips and tilted her head.

'What can you tell us about the cathedral outside? We visited it earlier, but still know little about it,' asked the slim redhead on the left.

Gigi looked at his interrogator. He was lucky that the only people in this backward town who knew less than him about its history were these two women. He took a long drag of his beer, playing for time, and planned his next move.

'Well, it has a fascinating story. And, of course, the building is very beautiful, like both of you,' said Gigi.

His words hung in the air. The silence was palpable. His heart raced as he glanced from one woman to the other, searching for any sign of a response. He'd committed himself now and would have to continue his spiel or leave with his tail between his legs. 'They built it in the sixteenth century, not only as a place of worship but also so the clock tower could be used as a warning system for advancing Milanese armies. I know the local priest, so if you stick with me, I can arrange for you to have a guided tour tomorrow, including all the areas that are out of bounds to ordinary people.' As he made his proposal, he leaned towards the brunette and winked.

'That's funny. We read it dates back to the fifteenth century, and the Milanese never came this far,' said Gigi's flame-haired accuser.

Gigi lifted the bottle to his mouth, keeping it there so as to hide his face.

'Well, I prefer your version,' said the brunette.

After a brief pause, the devil-haired woman burst out laughing and glanced at her watch. The only thing that prevented Gigi's blood from boiling over was the act of appraising the timepiece's value.

'Thank you for your offer, but we have a dinner reservation. You could be a gentleman and pick up these drinks, though,' said the brunette, before leaning in and kissing Gigi on the cheek.

As he opened his mouth to reply, the women rose from their seats and signalled to the barman where the bill should go.

Stunned at their audacity, Gigi could only watch them disappear. They left him with nothing but the faint, sickly smell of perfume to remember them by. His shoulders slumped forward, and he poured the rest of his beer down his throat. He stood up and shuffled back to the bar, ready for one more drink.

As the bottle arrived, so did the bill for the wine. Gigi sighed and hoped that he could fence the gear from the villa sooner rather than later. As he took out his wallet to pay for the drinks, a gentle touch on his arm made him turn.

Beside him was a young woman in a revealing black dress. She smiled.

'Fancy buying me a drink?'

Gigi knew he should decline. Just get back to the villa, grab the stuff and return to the city. His mind knew that, but his mouth ordered a couple of beers, and his legs took him to the table where the woman now sat. Her luscious right thigh on display for everyone to see.

The two of them sat facing each other. Gigi had lost the view of the woman's legs but gained an even better one down her dress as she leaned forward and grasped the top of the beer bottle. She rolled it around between her fingers before taking a small sip.

His jaw dropped lower than his companion's neckline, then he took a drink and the booze flowed like a waterfall down Gigi's throat.

'It looks like we're both on our own tonight,' said the woman.

'Your man stood you up?'

The woman looked Gigi in the eyes, fluttered her eyelashes, then smiled. 'What makes you think I have a man?'

'A beautiful woman like you must have a boyfriend, although I didn't notice a ring.' Gigi always noticed whether a woman had a ring. Not for any improper reason, but because it either meant a lot of money for him if he took it, or future disappointment for her, when she discovered it was worthless.

'Maybe you're about to change that,' said the woman.

A strange sound, a cross between a cough and a laugh, erupted out of Gigi's throat. He ran his fingers through his hair and glanced away.

'Oh, I've nearly finished my drink. Perhaps it's time for me to go,' said the woman. Her attention wandered to two men in suits who'd just entered. Gigi couldn't help but notice they returned the interest.

As the woman looked back at him, Gigi spotted the sadness in her eyes, as if she didn't want to leave. All he had to do was prove that he could provide for her, and she would be his. That's what his dad had told him, anyway. And for tonight, Gigi could pretend be that provider.

'I'll order us both another. Would you like a cigarette while I'm at the bar?'

'I thought that came after,' said the woman with a smile.

Gigi felt his cheeks turn hot. He shoved his hand into his trouser pockets and as he pulled out the crumpled pack made sure that the keys to the villa and the Ferrari fell onto the floor by her feet.

With a phony apology, he stooped down and retrieved them. As he straightened, he noticed the grin plastered across her face. His plan had worked.

'Is your Ferrari parked near here?'

'No, it's back at my place.'

'Oh. What's your place like?'

'Oh, you know, the usual out-of-town villa. Nothing too fancy. I think that showing off your wealth is quite vulgar,' said Gigi as he turned his head away, feigning modesty.

'Is it just you?'

'Yes, I guess I've been so caught up with business that I haven't had chance to meet the right woman. I have all these nice things, but without a woman's touch, the place doesn't seem like home.' The lies tumbled out of Gigi like coins in a winning slot machine. 'There's only so much one can own to fill the void when there's no companionship, isn't there?'

The woman agreed.

'Take my bed, for example. Silk sheets and fit for a king. But shamefully, one without a queen,' said Gigi, proud of his ever-rising level of smoothness.

'How about we get out of here and have that drink at yours?'

Gigi's heart worked double time as a particular organ demanded more of the blood flow. He finished the last of his drink, praying that the alcohol would drown any remaining common sense.

'I'll just pick up some more cigarettes, and then we can go,' said the woman as she stood up and sashayed to the bar. She leaned over the counter and said something to the barman before returning to the table. 'Are you ready to give me a ride?'

***

Gigi opened the passenger door, took the woman by the hand, and helped her out of the vehicle. Her cleavage flashed in front of his face, and he licked his lips. His sweaty paw squeezed her tight. She winced in pain.

'Easy, tiger. There's plenty of time for the rough stuff.'

Her comment made Gigi's skin burn. A strange combination of embarrassment and excitement sent a rush of dopamine through his body. He released her hand and slammed the door shut. His mind raced with possibilities. Lost in thought, he watched as the woman's mouth moved, but he heard no sound.

'I said, shall we?'

'Sure, whatever you want,' said Gigi, noting the look of impatience etched on her face.

The abrasive crunching of gravel underfoot replaced conversation, and each crackle increased the pressure in Gigi's mind. This was happening.

He was halfway up the stone steps to the front door when he realised she wasn't with him. His head snapped back, and his eyebrows pulled together. He turned and saw her standing at the bottom.

With that near-permanent smile on her face, her eyes followed the facade of the villa and flicked towards Gigi's groin. 'Wow, it's enormous.'

Gigi knew what he wanted to say but couldn't do it. Not just out of fear she'd have unrealistic expectations, or even because of embarrassment, though they were a part of it. No, it was because the less he said to mess up this situation, the better.

He cleared his throat and moved his hand, beckoning towards the door.

She sauntered up each step with deliberate slowness, her gaze lingering on Gigi until she was level with him. She paused before continuing on.

He remained transfixed by the sway of her hips and what jiggled beneath them.

She waited at the door with an expectant look on her face. 'Well, are you going to come here and get it out?'

Gigi stuttered an unintelligible response.

'The key,' she said.

Under her stare, he regained his composure as much as he could, bounded up the remaining steps and pulled out the keys. He shuffled them around, racking his brain to remember which it was. *Juventus!* He slid the key into the lock and, under his breath, prayed to Saint Cajetan, the patron saint of good fortune.

He was used to being under pressure when dealing with locks, but never had it caused him to sweat so profusely.

A satisfying click gave him a sense of relief almost comparable to what he hoped for later.

He pushed open the door and stepped aside.

The woman walked in, glanced around, and turned to face Gigi. 'Where's the little girls' room? I need to freshen up.'

A wave of nausea swept through his stomach and his head felt light. As he tried to speak, his throat tightened.

The woman stared at him for a moment then flashed a tight smile. 'I'll find it, don't worry. You just fix us some drinks and relax.' With that, she turned and headed up the stairs.

Alone in the hallway, Gigi breathed a sigh of relief. His body temperature returned to normal and, with it, rationality. He threw the keys into a little side bowl and rushed between doorways, peering inside each one in order to familiarise himself with the layout. In less than a minute, he was leaning against the living room door, gasping for breath and with beads of sweat dotted around his temples.

The creak of a floorboard overhead gave him a start. His body contorted, unable to keep up with his brain's desire to reach the kitchen. As his torso twisted one way, his leading foot turned another and slid back on the expensive rug that adorned the wooden floor. His arms flailed in front of him and his legs pumped like in an old cartoon, building momentum. Like a wound-up spring now released, he was propelled forward, face first and straight into the hallway table.

A loud and resonating boom reverberated off the walls as Gigi's forehead collided with the mahogany and sent him sprawling to the ground, where the back of his skull bounced off the hardwood floor.

The fuzzy sight of the beautiful art deco vase teetering on the edge of the table greeted him as his eyes stretched ever wider. Before he'd time to take a breath, the glassware grew larger and larger as it hurtled towards the large red bump that was forming on his forehead and acting like a bullseye.

He rolled to his side with milliseconds to spare as the expensive-looking vase smashed onto the floor.

After getting himself up, he stood over the scattered fragments and shook his head in disbelief. A week's worth of rent gone.

'Everything OK down there?'

'Yeah, don't worry about a thing. Take your time,' said Gigi, as he rubbed his forehead, thankful he had avoided any cuts. Using his foot, he slid the pieces of glass under the nearby table. He paused for a moment, spotting the briefcase, before continuing with a smile.

He stumbled into the kitchen, where he stopped at the black marble countertop on the far side. He shouted to his date to make herself at home in the living room.

'Do you have any music to put me in the mood?'

Shit. What does this asshole listen to? He would have guessed jazz or some other crap. Then Gigi had a more worrying thought. What happened if this jackass had pictures of himself or his wider family that he'd not spotted on that initial recce? He should have just turned the place over and got out. Why had he thought this was a good idea?

In the stillness that followed, Gigi could hear the low hum of modern appliances. He bit his lip and, unconsciously, his fingers tapped against the countertop. The bottle of J&B in the corner called to him. It invited him to drink. Drink, grab what he could, and run. Forget about the woman.

Then the cool voice of Adriano Celentano echoed throughout the house, and it saved him from answering the latest problematic question. He grabbed the whisky, a couple of tumblers, and searched for some ice. Giving up, he poured two generous helpings, downed one, and refilled his glass.

He cupped his hands to his mouth and checked his breath. Well, it was too late now. Then he unbuttoned the top five buttons of his shirt, picked up the drinks, and went to get what he deserved.

'Whisky?' Gigi asked, standing in the doorway.

The woman didn't respond. She just stared, as if seeing him for the first time. His heart sank as his fears appeared to have been realised.

'Are you OK?' she said.

'What do you mean?'

'Your head. There's a massive red mark... Never mind.'

She patted the opposite end of the sofa for him to sit on. It gave him a delightful view, so he didn't complain. They listened to the music, talked about themselves – all bullshit on his side – and continued to drink.

As each song ended, Gigi edged a little closer to the woman, but every time he tried to put his patented moves on her, she swerved all but the briefest of touches. The number of times she rose from the sofa for a top-up suggested to Gigi she might have a drink problem. Maybe that was her catch. Everyone had one. It explained why a woman like her was interested in him.

As the album finished, a low hum filled the room, and Gigi knew it was time to make a last grab for love.

His palms opened, his fingers moved into a cupping position and he turned his body, ready to embrace the beautiful creature beside him.

Fingers and fabric were centimetres away, while the mouths of the two soon-to-be lovers weren't far behind. Her scent was intoxicating, but that could have been the alcohol. At that moment, Gigi fell in love. His lips parted, and the anticipation built down below. He closed his eyes and waited for the loving connection.

A slender finger pressed on his lips instead.

'Finish your drink, then let's go upstairs,' she said.

Gigi squinted at the filled glass by his feet. He was certain he'd finished it a couple of tracks ago, but before doubt could take root, she spoke.

'That's a mighty big speaker you've got there,' purred the voice as a hand ran up his right leg. 'Now, drink up.'

Gigi downed the fiery liquid in one and prepared to get his prize, but her once smooth and delicate features had become hazy. Her body swayed like the branches of a tree in the wind.

His eyes blinked, his palms opened, and the glass spiralled down towards the floor.

An eternity passed before it shattered on a thin strip of exposed hardwood floor. Shards of alcohol-slathered glass flew under the sofa and across the deep shag carpet.

'My drink,' he slurred as his eyes shut.

The last thing he remembered was her smile.

***

'The bloody luggage,' mumbled Gigi as drool trickled down one side of his mouth.

He pushed himself up, his fingers clawing deep into the shag, and wiped the back of an arm across his eyes, displacing only the thickest of rheum. The rest filmed his vision in a blur.

Groaning, he looked around the sparse room. His mind tried to picture what was missing. The television. The stereo system. Some nice glass pieces from the mantelpiece. Had he put them in the car already?

As he was standing there, he heard a heavy thump emanating from the hallway.

'I'll have to catch another flight next week. If you can drop me off at the office, I'll get the details and call them to arrange. What the…'

The words swirled around in Gigi's head but made no sense. The putrid taste of bile filled his mouth as it rose from the pit of his stomach. He swallowed it back down and grimaced.

With a Herculean effort, he moved one leg forward, and then the other. Soon he was wading out of the room, across the hallway and into the kitchen in a desperate search for a glass of water.

'Who the…'

The words bounced off Gigi's thick skull as he continued towards the sink, where he turned the tap until cold liquid whooshed out and into his face. All the while, a bulldozer of a voice continued to push aggressive yet meaningless noise in his direction.

He patted his cheeks and exhaled before facing the source of the racket. A large, angry businessman in a crumpled suit.

'Who let you into my place?' said Gigi.

'Your place?'

Gigi turned and reached for a cupboard handle that wasn't there. His hand fell onto the marble countertop before his trembling fingers reached out for an invisible Moka pot.

The dishevelled executive resumed his foul-mouthed tirade and Gigi saw the walls of the villa shake. Or maybe they were still, and it was he who was moving. He stared at a blurred bottle of whisky and an empty vial next to it.

His hands dropped to his trousers and patted the pockets. At that moment, he felt like an impotent volcano. His body burned up inside, but with no outlet for his rage. His legs buckled, and he threw himself onto the counter to stop himself collapsing.

He squeezed his eyes shut, his forehead creased, and his head ached. After firing out three quick breaths, he hoped to see something different.

Everything was clearer, but nothing had changed. Veins in the red-faced client's neck bulged as he stood in the doorway. Fists were clenched at his sides. A grey-haired, bespectacled man in a cardigan and shirt waited behind him.

'I've been robbed,' muttered Gigi.

'You've been robbed?' the client spluttered, before turning back into the hallway. 'Luigi, call the police.'

Gigi followed and saw Luigi on the telephone, while the client searched the area, muttering something about business documents and keys.

Memories of the night came flooding back. Gigi patted down his pockets again and after coming up empty once more he sprinted toward the living room. With shaking hands, he threw the cushions into the air, shoved his fingers into every crevice of the sofa, and swept his arms underneath, begging for contact of any sort. With nothing to show for his efforts, he cursed the gods for what he now knew had happened.

He ran a clammy hand down his face and failed to stifle a tired sigh. This was always likely to happen. People used to joke that life hadn't given him a single lemon, but a whole grove. He had the type of luck that either killed you or turned you into an eternal optimist. Thankfully, he was the latter. That's why he still had hope.

Hope and a new Alfa.

Bathed in sweat, he burst out of the living room, down the hallway, past the two men, and out through the front door. He came to a sudden stop on the top step.

'No, no, no.'

Parked on the driveway was a brand new Mercedes. Nothing else.

'Where is it? What did you do with my car?' He stared blankly, as if seeing an optical illusion. After scrunching up his eyes and opening them again, he realised nothing was going to appear.

His head pounded like someone was drilling behind his sockets with a jackhammer.

As he used his thumb and index finger to wipe away the moisture from the corner of his eyes, a hand gripped his right shoulder, causing him to wince. 'The police will be here soon, and it looks like you aren't going anywhere,' said the voice.

It had only been one shift, but deep down Gigi knew it hadn't been the right job for him. But to go to jail for a crime he hadn't committed? No, that wasn't right.

He shrugged the hand off and ran down the steps, turning at the bottom. Thinking as fast as he could, he shoved his right hand into his jacket pocket and shaped his fingers like a gun. With his hand in his pocket and his eyes fixed on the homeowner, he began the long walk back to Torino.

'Don't move,' said Gigi. As he stepped backwards, his feet scuffed against the gravel and a square pebble lodged itself under his heel in his left shoe. It was going to be a long journey home.

Stolen Time

Gigi surveyed the endless line of people in front of him and let out an exasperated sigh. It had been at least five minutes since his feet had last moved in a forward direction, and the heat in the giant hall was stifling him.

Desperate for relief, he raised his flimsy pay cheque to his face and fanned himself. The sound of paper fluttered in his ears. Its movement, however, did little to ease his suffering.

He shoved the cheque back into his trouser pocket and untucked his shirt. The cheap polyester rustled, and the odour of dried sweat rose, filling his nostrils.

All this hassle for just ten thousand lire. With a shake of his head, he took another glance at the gaggle that blocked him from the clerk. He let out a loud disapproving sound and caught the attention of the young woman in front of him, who turned her head to look.

'In this heat you'd think they'd turn the air conditioning on, wouldn't you?' he said.

The attractive woman glanced at him dismissively and returned to minding her own business.

Faced with a lack of alternatives, Gigi reluctantly turned his attention to his surroundings. High ceilings, stone beams and more polished wood than a whorehouse. He smiled. His eyes scanned the pencil-necked managers in their cheap suits, the beautiful women at the counters, and a drowsy security guard by the door. Bank robbers had it easy these days.

Staring at the sloth-like guard, he thought back to when he'd tried to expand his criminal repertoire. It never worked out for him. No, he'd stick to commercial burglary and insurance jobs going forward. No victims. Not really.

As his gaze swept back across his fellow patrons, his eyes met a familiar sight. It was the man known as Molotov. Gigi didn't know his real name, and had never spoken to him, but everyone of a certain illegal persuasion knew his face and reputation. Today, however, he looked a little different. His hair was longer, and he had an unruly moustache that covered more area than it should have. Although nothing could hide the long scar that ran down the middle of his right eyebrow and below the eye. Rumour was, he received it in Rebbiba prison when three other inmates attacked him with shivs in the showers. He was the only one to walk away from the soapy chaos. At least that was the word on the street.

Gigi watched Molotov say something to the teller and then confidently approach the guard, now leaning against the wall by the entrance doors.

Low murmurs of boredom continued to echo around the great hall of finance, and Gigi turned, hoping to see some drama. He strained his neck and watched as one by one the people in front of him shuffled forward in a slow procession, filling the space vacated before them.

The hope of finally depositing his measly cheque made him contemplate his options, and how long the money would last. Not even a day, if his landlord caught up with him. Perhaps he should cash it out and take it down to the gambling dens. The way his luck was going, though, he was liable to lose it all. The phrase *winners never cheat, and cheaters never win*, ran through his mind.

No, he had to be more positive. He had learned his lesson, and this time he would hold his nerve. That would solve his current financial predicament. As he daydreamed, he pictured a shower of bank notes descending upon him as a line of women formed, all waiting for their chance to be his.

Without warning, his shoulders jerked down, and his fists tightened into a ball.

The sound of panic rang out and the air became infused with an acrid scent. Flakes of stucco floated to the ground, mimicking snowfall, and a high-pitched buzzing sound rattled around Gigi's skull, like a trapped bee desperate to escape.

Out of the corner of his eye he saw movement, but before he could turn, the body of the guard landed at his feet. Minus a small piece of his cranium. A thin, red liquid oozed out of the man's head, and crept towards Gigi's shoes. The thickening blood pursued him relentlessly, causing him to take a step back, and then another, until he bumped into the woman behind him with his elbow.

She looked at Gigi, then her eyes followed the blood to its source. Her face contorted, and a scream erupted out of her mouth. Gigi winced at the piercing tone, feeling it might rupture his eardrums.

'Quick. Sirens!' bellowed an imposing figure. His face was obscured by a menacing mask, and he stood guard by the door, clutching a deadly submachine gun in his grip.

Gigi's eyes darted from the masked man to Molotov. It was just the two of them he figured.

'We need a hostage,' replied Molotov. His heavy boots slapped against the marble floor as he raised his pistol and closed in on Gigi and the screaming woman.

'You, come here,' shouted Molotov. A finger raised at the lady.

Gigi's mind went blank as the volume of a police siren's two-tone wah-wah grew louder. It consumed his mind, blocking out any rational thought. Whether it was bravery or stupidity, he couldn't say, but he pushed the woman back, and in doing so, placed himself before the robber.

'Leave her alone,' Gigi blurted out before the barrel of a pistol filled his entire field of vision.

From over the gleaming metal. Gigi could see Molotov was eyeing up the woman as his preferred victim. It was obvious why. The police always acted more cautiously when it was a female hostage. At least until they knew what her family situation was like. But beyond that, Gigi knew the reality of someone like him. Expendable and with little value to either side.

An unintelligible grunt came from the huge masked watchman. Molotov removed his gun from Gigi's face and dropped it to his side. A sneer formed on his face.

Gigi watched the weapon sway in the man's loose grip. He could make a grab for it. Become a hero. His fingers twitched and his right leg bounced. Did he have the balls to take the gun?

He rocked gently back onto his heels and stretched his fingers out.

His head snapped forward, and instinctively he flung his arms out for balance and his feet struggled to maintain the enforced pace as rough, leather-gloved hands threw him towards the door.

Guttural screams of 'Fuckin' move' filled his eardrums. He was thankful nothing filled his trousers.

Without warning, the oppressive afternoon sun beat down on him, much like the fist that cracked into the right side of his ribs.

Doubled over, he gulped in the dry air and, through wet eyes, looked up at the shadowed figure of Molotov.

The next thing he knew, his shoes were scraping across the pavement as the gigantic gangster dragged him towards a black Alfa with the rear passenger doors open.

This was it, he thought. Heroes die and cowards live. Why did he have to get involved?

The giant flung Gigi headfirst into the back of the car before following him in.

Gigi crashed off the stone-like body of Molotov, already occupying the far seat.

His skin felt as cold as ice, causing the hairs on his arms and the back of his neck to stand on end. As he squirmed into an upright position, he took a breath, and consoled himself with the thought that as long as they needed a hostage, he would be safe.

Keeping his head facing forwards, Gigi turned his eyes and saw both men had their weapons pointed at him.

The roar of the engine drowned out his gulping.

'You got the cash?' said Molotov.

'In the boot,' said the large man as he pulled his mask off, revealing a tanned, chiselled face.

With a deafening roar of the engine, the car lunged forward, carving its way through the sparse traffic, leaving the police in the rear-view mirror arriving to find only the smear of burned rubber on tarmac.

'Who the hell is this prick?' spat the large man, looking at Gigi. 'Where's the woman? It's better to have a woman like last time.'

'I tried, but this asshole got in the way and there was no time to get anyone else. He'll do as a speed bump for any cops, though,' said Molotov with a grin.

A shrill laugh burst out of Gigi's mouth, causing the two robbers to scowl at him. All he could do was flash an apologetic smile in return. Inside, though, his thoughts screamed at him. *This would not end well.*

He thought about who to blame. These thugs, of course, but beyond them the catalyst for all of this was that bloody chauffeur job. Trying to earn an honest pay cheque was the worst decision he ever made.

Taking another sideways glance, he wondered if he should try to reason with the men? After all, they were all professional criminals. But these turbulent times had taught him many things. It wasn't just mainstream society that was in upheaval, but the underworld, too.

The old ways were dying out, much like their guardians. Youngsters nowadays were a different breed of criminal, and these men were certainly from the new school. Violence had replaced honour. The code of *omertà* was foreign to them. Instead, they liked to ensure silence with a bullet.

With a sagging of his shoulders, Gigi accepted his fate and stared blankly at the city passing by outside the window, where the buildings and the people merged into a head-splitting blur.

As the vehicle turned left off the nondescript main road and over a bridge, a glimpse of shimmering water caught Gigi's attention. The River Po. They emerged into the tree-lined Piazza Muzio Scevola. Not that he could recall it.

'I think we're clear. Should we throw him out before the autostrada?' said the brute, as he poked the barrel of his gun into Gigi's ribs.

'Quiet. We aren't safe yet,' said Molotov as he turned to look behind.

It was then Gigi heard it. For once in his life, he felt elation at the sound of a police siren.

Two vehicles tore across the bridge and thundered into the piazza amid a chorus of car horns. Their sirens wailed like banshees, giving pursuit to their prey.

Gigi's heart pounded, and his hands became slick with sweat. Instinctively, he checked the exits. He had no hope.

As the getaway vehicle reached the wide road of the Corso Monterotondo, the pursuing vehicles split up. A classic pincer movement. The first charged across the grass bank, weaving through the looming poplar trees as it attempted to overtake and cut up the thieves' car, while the second maintained its relentless pursuit but edged slightly to the getaway vehicle's right.

Cursing, the driver swung the wheel right and then left, causing each large man in the back to take turns sliding into Gigi, crushing him against the bulk of the other large man.

As the air returned to his lungs, and the last of the moisture left his eyes, Gigi stole another look at his travelling companions. Their tightened faces showed no emotion. But their hands readied their weapons.

In a firefight, he'd be a sitting duck.

He placed his hands on his quivering knees, desperately attempting to steady them.

The car's tyres screeched as it turned a corner hard, causing the back end to fishtail. The driver regained control and raced down the long Corso Moncalieri, ignoring the steep first left turn and putting distance between them and the pursuing vehicles.

'What are you doing? They'll set up a roadblock, you idiot.'

The car roared past the blue facade of the crumbling Teatro Erba, where garishly costumed thespians stood with their mouths agape at the free spectacle unfolding before them.

'I've got it,' said the driver, now hunched forward. Eyes narrowed.

'You better get us to Pessione, else it'll be a bullet for you,' said Molotov. The almost floral alcohol on the man's breath filled the rear of the car and sent Gigi's mind back to when he had a family. To a nonna who drank too much Martini, and a front room reeking of vermouth for days after one of her sessions.

Inside the vehicle, the deafening roar of an engine being pushed beyond its limit drowned out all other sound. The speedometer climbed higher and higher.

Trapped within the confines of the metallic cocoon, the oppressive tension weighed down on Gigi, making it difficult to breathe. The muscles in his limbs twitched with nervous energy. He knew the others felt the same.

'Fuck!' said the driver, as the police cars converged and grew in the rear-view mirror.

Gigi narrowed his eyes and craned his neck to see.

Then he looked up at the rusty roof and smiled. *Grazie a Dio.*

The sound of Molotov's fist meeting the thin metallic roof echoed through the vehicle, filling the air with a sharp thud. '*Cazzo!*' he shouted.

Gigi's smile turned sideways as his neck contracted and someone knocked the wind out of his stomach. Unfortunately for everyone involved, it didn't come out of his mouth.

He squeezed his eyes shut as his body contorted and rolled forward. A biting wind attacked his face, slapping it with an icy hand, as rough tarmac tore away at his clothes and skin. The word *stronzo* hung in the air.

As the world gradually snapped into focus, a searing pain shot down his body. He groaned, his palms pressed against the ground, the rough surface scraping against his skin like sandpaper.

With a grunt, he pushed himself up, his head barely clearing the floor. His gaze locked onto the barrel of a Carabinieri rifle, sending a chill down his spine.

'I'm innocent,' he said, before his head crashed down onto the road.

In the distance, the getaway car mounted the pavement and turned down the narrow Strada del Fioccardo, bouncing off a Fiat 500 as it hurtled towards safety.

***

As the naked lightbulb swung back and forth, Gigi raised a hand to his left temple and squeezed his eyes shut, desperate to stem the piercing pain that had built behind his retinas.

He placed his hands on the table and fired out a series of breaths. His wrists still ached from the tight handcuffs that had been snapped on during his trip to the station, while his skin remained raw from where he'd skidded across the road. He felt like shit, and that was before the famed police hospitality had even begun.

The door to the interrogation room opened and a stocky pale man in a crumpled brown suit walked in. His gaze locked onto Gigi as he grabbed the bulb from the air in one meaty hand, leaving it motionless, and then departed.

This type of treatment wasn't new to Gigi, so he continued to wait. He closed his eyes and focused on his breathing.

'Wake up, you stupid bastard,' said a gruff voice.

Gigi cursed the Madonna under his breath. He was certain the door hadn't opened. Yet, somehow, the same translucent bully from before was now sitting opposite him.

The apparition introduced himself as Inspector Fano and offered Gigi a cup of coffee.

Gigi downed the thick syrup in one. He didn't say thank you. Not because he was ungrateful or that it tasted like shit, but because it was an insincere attempt to butter him up.

'Why'd they throw you out of the car? A misunderstanding about the split?' said the inspector.

Thoughts darted around Gigi's brain like frenzied butterflies, fluttering and colliding but never settling. He tried to answer, but the words came out jumbled, as if he'd just thrown them onto the table like dice in a game of craps.

The inspector stared at him and the word garbage that he'd spewed out.

Whether it was the coffee, the room or something else, Gigi felt the pores in his skin close over and his body temperature rising. 'I'm the victim here! I should be in the hospital, not in a cell. Those bastards threw me from a moving car.'

'And who are they? Don't plead innocence, Gianluigi Moretti. I've seen your file. I must admit, though, this was a step up for you. Perhaps you tried to play with the big boys and got burned? They used your skills, then discarded you. If you admit your guilt, and give me their names, I'll have a word with my pal, the prosecutor, and have him go easy on you. What do you say?'

The faces of the two robbers flashed before Gigi's eyes. Images of the violence they could inflict on him followed and sent a shiver down his spine. Taking a moment to compose himself, he inhaled deeply before answering. He was innocent, so there was no harm in telling the truth. A selective version of it, anyway.

'They wore masks. I couldn't even pick them out in a line-up,' said Gigi. He hoped he had lied convincingly.

As the inspector sighed, an unwelcome waft of cured ham made its way across the table and into Gigi's face. How long had it been since *he* last ate?

The inspector rose out of his chair and walked over to the door. He rapped on it twice with calloused knuckles. It cracked open slightly, and the inspector muttered something to the man on the other side before turning back to Gigi. 'I can keep you for twenty-four hours. So, I will. Give you opportunity to remember some details.'

'I know my rights. I should have a lawyer.'

'One is on their way, but what with the traffic in this city...' said the inspector, casually waving a hand. 'Relax and enjoy your stay.'

***

The time passed quickly. Although Gigi didn't have any cellmates to talk to, it meant he could get a decent stretch of sleep. At seven in the morning they hauled him back into the concrete box and asked the same questions again.

Gigi stonewalled every pertinent question about the robbery, and in return had to witness a diatribe against his way of living, and the current state of society.

'OK, Moretti, you've had your chance to save your skin. Now it's your mate's turn.'

Gigi's forehead creased, and he stared at the inspector, unable to comprehend the meaning behind the words.

'Oh, didn't I say? We picked up your pal, the getaway driver. Stupid bastard took a joyride and got himself pinched. My offer still stands, though. Whoever confesses first gets the leniency. Think it over.'

The inspector left the room and a few minutes later an officer escorted Gigi out and processed him for release.

***

BORN TO LOSE

Gigi stood at the corner of Corso Racconigi and Via Envie and glanced up and down the empty streets. He usually loved August. It was a time when the offices were closed, and the people fled the city for the beaches. A commercial thief's paradise. This summer was different, however. The extreme heatwave had made his usual work attire itchy, and now, because of this situation, things were only going to get hotter.

The sun was rising, and it would take him fifty minutes to walk back to his apartment in Valdocco. He rummaged around in his pockets and counted his change. There was barely enough for a bus ticket.

As he stifled a yawn, his brain screamed at him for caffeine. No doubt his body would appreciate the energy boost, too. He set off and, were it not for the small mercy of the tall buildings surrounding him, he would have melted before he even reached the bar on the edge of the wide Piazza Sabontino.

Seeking refuge from the rising heat, he counted each coin out and ordered a glass of water and an espresso. Then he headed over to the payphone on the wall, dropped a token into the machine and dialled his old friend, Ciuccio.

He didn't know why he was calling, only that he wanted to vent.

'Ciuccio, it's me.'

'Gigi? You got problems, pal. First, Ranieri is getting cold feet about you doing that industrial job.'

'Yeah, so am I.'

'That's not the issue, though.'

'Why? I've been locked up all night. Only this time I'm innocent, I swear. You know that bank robbery in San Donato? Well, that bastard Molotov did it. Then him and his goons took me for a joy ride before throwing me out in front of the cops. They're trying to pin it on me, so I'm a marked man, and can't risk working. But I've no money and need to borrow some.'

'I've no cash either. Sorry, pal. Maybe I can still help, though.'

'What, you going to pay my landlord with your body? Thanks, but I think that might drive my rent up.'

'Shut up. As I was saying, you've got bigger problems. Word has spread about your shacking up with the pigs. And that robbery you weren't involved in? Well, a little birdie told me the police are picking them all up as we speak. Rumour is they've already stashed the money, though. Playing the long game. Worst-case scenario, they live off the state for a few years, get out and collect their pay day then. Over half a million lire. Imagine that.'

Gigi whistled down the line. 'You reckon they'll go down?'

'You better hope they do. As, for you getting picked up first, the word is that you've started scuttling round the streets, saving your own skin. If you catch my drift?'

'Me? I'm no rat. It was that stupid driver of theirs. Fuck!'

'Probably. But if Molotov gets out, he's going to come looking for you. Especially now he's lost that cushy day job of his because of the attention this brought him. Maybe you should take a holiday.'

'A holiday? I don't even have the money to get the bus in this shit city. I gotta go.'

Before waiting for a response, Gigi hung up and went to the bar. He downed his coffee and thought about what Ciuccio said. Him. A rat? That was the death knell for someone in his line of work. You didn't have a CV or a portfolio to share with clients. You only had your reputation, and when that was gone, so was your livelihood.

Sure, he could move away, but reputations were like an unpleasant smell. They followed you around. As he ordered a second drink, he flirted with the idea of going straight. He shook his head. That's what got him into this mess in the first place. No, he needed another solution.

He downed the bitter liquid and headed off home. If people suspected him of being in bed with the police, then it was best he avoid his usual haunts. Whether that made him look guilty didn't matter. It kept him alive.

***

His stomach growled as once again he found himself sat in the same pokey, metallic chair as before, as the idiotic inspector tried a different mind game. This time it was the silent treatment.

In the room's stillness, Gigi slumped down. He thought back to that morning. The loud banging on his apartment door. Its hinges rattling with every thump. And the brutal treatment employed to bring him down to the station. Only a friendly chat, they'd said. The bruises on his cheek showed just how friendly.

For five minutes, neither man said a word.

Gigi spotted a twitch under the inspector's right eye and tensed his jaw to stifle a smile.

With a deep sigh, the officer placed both hands on the table and leaned forward. 'Save us all some time and admit it.'

Gigi stared at the adversary and remained silent. He was happy enough to be the victor in this petty little match.

'Sure, you weren't the brains behind it. Anyone could see that. Your mates said you were thick as shit. Looking at your dumb ass, I agree. I'll bet they forced you along and then, when they'd had enough, threw you out of the car like a piece of rubbish. You aren't friends. Give me their names.'

Gigi smiled. He wasn't a genius by any stretch, but he also wasn't the idiot this guy thought he was. He was just unlucky. Often. Then his smile disappeared, and he remembered what happened to his old mentor, Moggi. The state police hadn't needed to prove his guilt, only his lack of innocence.

The air in the room became fetid as stale coffee and cigarettes mingled with the sort of stench that only a long shift and a scorching sun can produce. Gigi's nose wrinkled.

'It's written all over your face. You were in the bank. You were in the getaway vehicle. You're a bloody career criminal. All we want from you now is to stop wasting everyone's time and tell us your side of the story. Give names and sign a confession!'

The veins on the inspector's neck bulged as he stood up and strolled behind Gigi, who used every muscle in his neck to keep his head facing forward.

'You shouldn't be talking to me without a lawyer. You have no right to hold me,' said Gigi.

'I'll let you go all right. In a minute, you'll be free to scamper all over the city like the rodent you are.'

'I'm no rat.'

'That doesn't matter, because I'm putting the word out that you squealed in order to get off. My informants are spreading the news as we speak. Don't worry, though. One call from me, and they can end the misunderstanding.'

'People won't believe it,' said Gigi, knowing the damage would already have been done.

'But will they ever trust you again?' said the inspector, as if reading Gigi's thoughts. He shuffled to the door and opened it. 'You're free to go, but let me tell you one more thing. If you don't give me what I want, I'll be cutting your pal Molotov loose in a couple of hours and I might accidentally drop your name into conversation.'

***

Outside the station, Gigi's right hand tapped against his thigh as his nervous system and his cortex wrestled between whether to fight or flee. A dull ache formed in his temples and moved behind his eyes as the situation combined with the oppressive sun to squeeze his brain.

He ran a hand down his dry face, stretching the tight skin, and leaving a burning sensation where his fingers had been. Hypothetical situations continued to crash against each other in his throbbing skull. These worries intensified, building up like the nausea deep inside him.

Placing a hand against the hot brick, he leaned forward and exhaled.

Knowing that time was against him, Gigi realised that to get out of this mess, he would need to think logically. Although if what the inspector said was true, then the decision had already been made for him.

What option was there but to get the hell away from Torino?

The fact he would have to begin again with nothing didn't matter. He'd spent his entire life in this city, and what did he have to show for it? *Niente.*

With a slight nod of his head, he decided on a plan. Grab some clothes, nab a car and head to his cousins in Genoa. Easy.

He hurried along the streets, each step taken with purpose. His mind focused and replaying his task list. Clothes. Car. Genoa. Clothes. Car. Martini.

Indecision crept up on him and as he reached an intersection, the rapid neon flash of a sign in a nearby window called out to him. He stepped down off the curb before the blast of a horn sent him straight back again.

A cream Fiat 500 hurtled past, its horn blaring again as it sped off into the distance. But Gigi didn't pay it any attention. He remained transfixed by the flashing red and white logo on a black background. The light flickered a few more times before it died.

It was very much like Gigi's opportunities. Since childhood, he'd been unlucky. He'd worked hard in school, scoring well in tests, but when his parents got ill, he had to work instead of taking his final exams.

Despite lacking any formal qualifications, he secured an apprenticeship and soon rose to become a master locksmith, but just as he was about to inherit the business, his boss's estranged son moved back and took it away from him. It seemed each time he found a bit of happiness for himself, fate intervened. It was all downhill from there.

At least until now. That flickering light in the window had done more than entice him in. It had given him an idea, and if his hunch was right, he was about to call in every one of these debts.

Stepping through the air-conditioned entrance of the bar, he ordered two *bignoline* pastries with an espresso and hoovered them down. With sugar and caffeine coursing through his veins, he skipped out on the bill and headed home with new plan.

***

He checked both sides of the narrow alleyway before popping the boot of the car and throwing in a couple of small suitcases. After taking another look to make sure the coast was clear, he hopped behind the wheel and pressed the two exposed wires together.

By the time he reached the motorway, his muscles had relaxed and colour returned to his knuckles. A ray of sunshine caught his face, while the wind blew in through a crack in the driver's side window and raced through his hair. He felt good. Certain that soon he was going to be starting a new life. A better life.

He continued driving for thirty minutes, ignoring the small towns that dotted his path, until he passed Chieri, a place famed for its rich focaccia. His thoughts drifted to those summers he spent as a youth on the Genoese coast. It was ironic that those sweet memories involved a saltier regional focaccia.

Soon the town, like those experiences, was in the rear view and Gigi continued to a rural road that headed towards the village of Pessione.

Confident that he hadn't been tailed, either by the law or anyone else, he pulled up outside a plain bar on the far side of Piazza Luigi Rossi. The brickwork was crumbling, and the keystone above the door had seen better days. The inscription was so faint that, even when squinting, he couldn't make out the words. It didn't matter; the place was a dump with a filthy espresso machine, but he would still have chosen it.

He entered the grimy bar, paid, and then waited at the counter. Within a matter of seconds, a saucer and spoon were slung onto the counter before him and seconds after that, a porcelain cup filled with the elixir of life. He drank it in two sips, bummed a telephone token from the barista, and went to make his call.

'Ciuccio, it's me. Never mind where I am. One question. Molotov has been sacked, right?'

Gigi smiled as he looked out of the window at the Casa Martini sign opposite.

After begrudgingly paying for the drink – he couldn't afford any drama – he strolled past the two small gates of the Martini building.

Then he crossed the road and loitered for a couple of minutes outside the ticket office of the train station. There, he dumped his bags in a locker and doubled back on himself before walking through the open entrance gate.

Gigi paused for a second and took in the stylish Casa Martini, a large white brick building with three small balconies and one large one. He noted the immaculate state of the shutters on both floors. There was no possibility of a night-time search of the place. Even if he knew what he was looking for, the entire location was well-maintained, and that meant people paid attention. In his years of experience, the best way to do a job like this was in plain sight.

After completing his inspection of the perimeter, he marvelled at the intricate design of the main building's circular entrance, including the two majestic staircases that flanked it. He noted every detail as he considered his next move.

'Can I help you? Do you have an appointment or a booking?'

Gigi turned and saw a young woman in a black and red striped dress standing by the main door. A mixture of concern and expectation was on her face.

Transfixed by her beauty, his voice wobbled as he made his gambit. 'I've been told there's a vacancy here.'

She sighed before raising a hand to beckon him to follow. 'This way.'

They walked down a worn path that led away from the grand building and the people with money.

'You're in luck. We've just let one of our labourers go,' she said, tossing the words out with notable disdain. '*Massimo!*'

With that call, she returned to her palace of pretension. Gigi watched as she trotted away.

Massimo cleared his throat. 'Like what you see?'

'Yeah,' said Gigi absentmindedly. 'I, er, heard there was a vacancy.'

'You and everybody else, it seems. You're the second person today to come here asking around. He quit after an hour, so I hope you stick around longer. What's strange is that I haven't even told anyone there's an opening.' The man's eyes narrowed. 'The last guy I had work for me was a wrong 'un. You look the same. But he was a bloody good worker when he was here, so I'll take a chance.' The man threw a shovel towards Gigi. 'Besides, there's a big event tomorrow, and I'm running out of time. The greenhouse and work shed are down there. Go grab some fertiliser and make a start digging up the cleared area down the bottom.'

Before Gigi could reply, Massimo had gone back into his own little outbuilding and shut the door.

Confused at how he'd ended up being a groundsman instead of a rich outlaw, Gigi shuffled down the path and into a large wooden shed. Dirty espresso cups and men's magazines, along with metal toolboxes, loose pliers, and shears, littered the far workbench, while various wooden containers and several bags of seeds and fertiliser were stored underneath.

In the quiet of the hut, Gigi stared at the mess. Maybe he was going about things all wrong. He wanted a fresh start. And here it was. Sure, it wasn't living it up on the Ligurian coast with babes and booze, but it was something. After all, there was alcohol nearby, and that woman who brought him here: well.

Surveying his new kingdom, he nodded in contentment and smiled. Crossing the room, he pulled out a foldout chair and collapsed down into it. The rusted metal legs creaked slightly as they adjusted to his weight.

The place stank, but if he tossed the dirty cups and kept the mags, it might be quite nice here. A private kingdom. He would need to investigate what was in all the boxes, though, and sell what he could get away with.

Happily resigned to his new life, Gigi hauled himself out of the seat and appraised the containers. As he crouched down, pulling a box out, a slither of light caught his attention. Deep wrinkles formed across his forehead as his eyes narrowed and he moved in for a closer inspection. In the far corner, beneath another untidy bench, the floorboard had been raised. Not much, but enough so it had separated from the walls of the unit, letting a bit of sunshine in.

Gigi glanced back at the door, straining to catch even the slightest sound, causing his jaw and neck to throb with tension. Satisfied that no one would interrupt him, he crawled over and pulled up the board.

The wood creaked and bent before eventually yielding to his curiosity. With a snap, the far end splintered, and Gigi threw it behind him.

If it turned out to be nothing but woodlice and dirt, then he could cover the gap with a box and Massimo would be none the wiser.

His eyes strained, seeking to adapt to the darkness below. One thing was certain. It wasn't some natural quirk in the ground. Someone had dug this hole, but who – and why?

He shuffled slightly to the side and yanked a bit more of the wooden board away, his eyes adjusting to the dark little corner he occupied.

'Come on, a man's got to work!' Massimo's loud voice carried on the wind and practically blew the flimsy shed door open.

Gigi sprung to his feet and the top of his head crashed against the underside of the table, sending him back down onto the dirty floor.

He scuttled towards the entrance, where he stood and pressed the side of his face against a grime-encrusted window just in time to spot the inspector walking in his direction. Trailing behind him was a uniformed officer and a protesting Massimo. Ignoring the squished remnants of bugs and dirt, Gigi placed his other cheek against the glass and looked for an escape route beyond the shed.

Then he rushed back to the hole, dropped to the floor and forcefully inserted his hand, determined to find what was inside.

Meanwhile, outside, Massimo's irritation grew louder, and the flimsy, single-paned windows rattled. 'Come on, come on,' muttered Gigi as his hands pushed deeper, stopping only when his fingers grazed firm leather. His fingers explored the material before wrapping around a handle.

'Got you,' said Gigi, before yanking the bag up, followed by two more. Leaving them on the floor, he grabbed as many boxes and chairs as he could and dumped them behind the door before returning to his loot.

The conversation outside grew louder.

Gigi stretched his hands along the bottom panels of the wall and pulled with all his might. The crack filled his eardrums, and the force of his effort sent him onto his back. Without thinking, he twisted his body, scooped the three bags up, and bundled himself towards the gap.

Splinters dug into his soft midsection and broken pieces of wood scraped along his torso and limbs as he wriggled through the narrow space. His trailing foot made it through as the door opened outwards and confusion flowed from Massimo's mouth as to the state of his shed and the whereabouts of his new recruit.

Mud sprayed out from under Gigi's boots as he slid through the soil and burst out from behind a mass of green foliage and headed towards the bottom of the garden.

In the distance, he could hear a commotion. If they caught him, he may as well have robbed the bank himself. Innocent people don't run, and they certainly aren't found in possession of stolen money.

Trailing mud and leaves behind him, Gigi followed the gravelled path until it went off at a right angle.

Panting hard, he took a moment to consider his choices: to follow the route and head back towards the house or to scale the eight-foot brick wall looming over him.

Massimo's loud voice continued to fill the garden.

Dropping two bags, Gigi swung the remaining one between his legs. Once he'd built up enough momentum, he launched it into the air and over the wall. It was only then that he thought about what he was doing. Not the illegality, that was beyond question, but who or what was on the other side?

'Hello?' he said, before allowing a beat to pass and throwing the remaining bags over.

Then he took two steps back and launched himself at the wall.

His arms extended and fingers stretched out desperately. The clouds in the sky crowded round and watched. With a sickening thud, Gigi's chin met the unforgiving cold of the brick, and he plummeted into the dirt below.

'He must be somewhere,' said Massimo.

The voices were getting nearer.

After picking himself up, Gigi dusted himself down and glanced around for something he could use. A ladder. A bin. Anything. He threw up his arms, and they dropped almost immediately.

He turned in a circle, scratched his head, and exhaled. There was nothing except for beautiful plants and forgettable trees. Trees that stood taller than eight feet.

Throwing himself at the trunk of the closest one, Gigi shimmied up, hugging it like a young monkey on its mother, until he reached a suitable height. Satisfied, he shuffled along a large branch, and without checking if it could take the impact, pushed down, and launched himself off and into the unknown.

The makeshift catapult sent him over the wall, but he had overshot and hurtled down towards the road at a speed his brain couldn't comprehend. With his arms and legs spread, he resembled a cat falling. But without the balance.

His tender skin cracked on the impact, and the old wounds opened as he crashed onto the hard surface. A sharp pain exploded out from his elbows. He closed his eyes, rolled to the side, and over the painted white line that marked the pavement.

He laid on his back for a moment, staring up at the blue sky above him. The mocking clouds had moved on after their entertainment. His breathing had increased in pitch and frequency until erupting into laughter at the touch of the three bags by his side.

Now standing with the loot in hand, Gigi glanced down the road, towards the train station and his locker, and the adjacent corner leading to the entrance of Casa Martini. There was no sense in heading back. So, he said goodbye to his few belongings, and headed towards the motorway, leather bags swinging by his side, where he'd attempt to flag down a lift to the next town, and then on to Genoa.

***

It took less than five minutes before an old man, with more hair sprouting out of his nose than his head, picked Gigi up and drove him all the way to the city of Asti.

The man dropped Gigi off at the coach station. His muttered words about sticking it to the fascists lingered in the air as he vanished in a plume of black smoke.

Gigi cleared his throat and waved away the thick fumes. He looked around the area, then picked up his bags of loot and waddled into the only visible shop.

Inside, the shopkeeper's suspicious gaze followed his every move, and he noticed them narrow as he withdrew some notes from one of his bags.

With little more than a perfunctory interaction, Gigi left with their most expensive suitcase.

After a quick detour to the public toilets, where he shoved the rest of his money into his new purchase, turning it into a portable bank, he went and bought a one-way ticket to Genoa.

Despite the uneventful twenty-minute wait on the stop, Gigi remained on high alert. He scrutinised every passenger, passer-by, and employee. Everyone was a potential cop, or worse, a criminal. He didn't think it a stretch of the imagination to believe that word of his defection to the other side, or even his theft of the money, had travelled this far.

But there was nothing he could do about it now. Just wait in line. Not attract any attention. Over the shoulder of the person in front of him he saw the headlines. Something about the perpetrators of the Marazzi kidnapping still being at large. Then the man turned the page to financial news and Gigi lost interest. That killed about a minute.

His right leg trembled as he stared at the clock that jutted out from the station's entrance. Its hands were moving so slowly as to almost defy time itself.

When the coach pulled up, his body was slick with sweat, and his head pounded.

He clambered on board, walked halfway down the narrow aisle, and dropped the suitcase on the window seat before sitting down next to it. It would be foolish to leave half a million lire in the hold. You couldn't trust anyone these days.

After everyone took their seats, the engine rumbled, and they headed off.

For the next thirty minutes, the trip was uneventful. The rowdy group of teenagers filling the back seats quietened down, and the other passengers maintained a respectful silence or, at the very most, quiet conversation.

Gigi breathed a sigh of relief. In under three hours, he would be in Genoa, ready to start again. The thought made him smile. He glanced out of the window and stared as the distant greenery went by in a blur, resembling an Impressionist painting he once saw at the Galleria Sabauda when he was a child.

A thick, acrid scent of oil soon accompanied the memory. The smell pervaded the coach, along with a deep, rumbling vibration that caused the nuts and bolts in Gigi's seat to rattle under the growing pressure. A thunderous boom echoed down the vehicle and was joined by a crescendo of car horns surrounding the coach in a sea of noise.

The coach shuddered onwards as Gigi grabbed the tattered headrest of the seat in front of him, stood up, and looked around. His gaze was drawn to the elderly woman sitting in the opposite row. Her shawl framed the confusion etched on her face. Unsure what to do, Gigi looked into her wide eyes, and provided his most comforting smile. In return, she curled her lips and turned away.

Voices became raised all around him as accusations were aimed at the red brigades or the fascists, depending on their owners' political leanings.

'Calm down, everyone, it's just a flat tyre. There's a petrol station up ahead. Let's see if we can make it,' said the baritone voice of the driver. His almost bored manner did little to quell the conspiracy theorists around Gigi.

The bus tilted to the left and crept onwards for another five minutes before lumbering into the motorway service station.

'Everyone off,' said the driver in a resigned tone before opening the doors and departing without a care for his passengers.

Gigi grabbed his suitcase, placed himself between two elderly people, and shuffled off the coach with them. All the while, his eyes darted around his fellow passengers to see if anyone looked suspicious. Considering the amount of money involved, he wouldn't have been surprised if this was a setup.

Huddled together on the asphalt next to the bus, the gaggle of travellers surrounded the driver, who nonchalantly pulled out a cigarette from his trouser pocket and lit up.

Amid a barrage of questions, he at least had the decency to blow the smoke into the air while ignoring the worries of his charges.

When he'd finished what Gigi assumed to be his mandated break, the driver threw down the remnants of the cigarette and placed his hands up.

'Calm down, people, this happens all the time. I'll phone the depot and they'll send a replacement. It's no big deal. In the meantime, go to the station, or stretch your legs. Whatever you want.'

His attempt to placate the crowd riled them up, and accusations of laziness coupled with incompetence flew around.

By now, Gigi had decided that no one was out to get him. And free of that burden, he took a deep breath. The foul air, made up more of petrol fume than oxygen, caused him to cough. Once he recovered, he noticed a stale scent that was closer than any vehicle. He dropped his head to his chest and smelt again. His face recoiled at the pungent aroma coming off his shirt.

Suitcase in tow, he headed towards the service station. If he had to spend some time here, he may as well use it to make himself presentable. A man with money needed to look the part.

After years of trying to make something of his life, both within and without the law, he chuckled at the fact that it was someone else's efforts that had finally seen him get rich. His even footsteps continued as his mind wandered into the future. Maybe he'd go straight again. The previous times hadn't worked because he had no start-up capital. That was all he needed. A little luck and seed money. He could become a legitimate businessman. Use the money to set himself up in Genoa.

Although his eyes remained fixed on the station before him, his mind pictured the store. His store. He would have an elegant sign outside stating his name, and attract the affluent Genoese. It would be tastefully decorated inside and sell a variety of state-of-the-art home security measures. The latest stuff from America. Business would be thriving. He'd be a respected member of society. Get a good woman with her own money. One who wouldn't ditch him when times were tough or, more likely, a handsome face looked her way.

'Watch it, comrade,' said a voice with a chuckle.

Gigi stumbled, and his suitcase toppled over on its front. He ducked down to lift it up and then glared towards the man who'd startled him.

The highway police officer towered over him.

Gigi swallowed the rock in his throat and stole a look back at the coach.

'You part of the coach group?' said the officer, following Gigi's gaze.

Gigi did his best to level his voice and answer yes.

'Where are you headed?'

Now keeping his head straight, Gigi couldn't stop his eyes from shifting side to side. What did this man want from him? Did he know? No, that was impossible.

Gigi opened his mouth but, before he could reply, the officer's colleague came over and whispered in his ear. The two men stared at Gigi for a moment before heading to their vehicle, which was parked by the entrance to the service building.

Biting his lip, Gigi gripped the handle of his luggage hard and stormed back to the coach. He approached the driver, who was smoking another cigarette, and asked for an update.

'Well, given how far we've come, and the schedules, and as you know there's a lack of drivers, then I think after I phone them, they'll be here in an hour. Possibly two.'

'An hour from now?'

'No, from when I call them.'

An exasperated sigh exploded out of Gigi's mouth and he threw his hands up in the air, causing his suitcase to crash to the floor for a second time. He rubbed his chin with a damp hand and looked around.

It was then he saw it. A rust-and-red Lancia Beta convertible with its top down.

After thanking the driver for all his help, he picked up his suitcase and walked stiffly to the vehicle.

He'd made it about halfway before the two highway officers strolled out of the service station, each with a small plastic cup. Standing out in the open, Gigi felt exposed. He had nowhere to hide and if he moved too quickly, he risked catching their attention and suspicion. No cop needed a reason to bring you in or even fire at you. Not since the implementation of the Reale Law, which gave them the right to shoot first and ask questions later.

Gigi stood like a statue and waited. He didn't want to risk standing out and blowing his future

'Hey, buddy,' said the driver.

Gigi turned round to see the man wave him over and in doing so missed the officers strolling around the Lancia.

'So, my shift has actually ended and because I'm a real nice guy and all, I thought I'd let you know the next bus won't be here for another couple of hours. And that one will take you back to Torino.'

Gigi spluttered something resembling words. He couldn't go back to Torino. No way. He turned around. The Lancia was still there. Bursting into action, his legs pumped back and forth as his luggage bounced off the smooth concrete, struggling to keep up.

When he reached the car, his right arm ached from dragging the heavy piece of luggage, but he dug deep, grunted and threw the luggage into the rear seats. With a level of dexterity that lent itself to the term cat burglar, he launched himself over the door and into the driver's side from where he set about pulling out the wires that controlled the ignition.

Less than a minute later, the engine roared to life with a fierce growl. The car shot backward, tyres shrieking against the asphalt, as Gigi slammed the gearshift and the car rocketed onto the autostrada, leaving a trail of burnt rubber and adrenalin in its wake.

Inside the station, Officer Giraldi was on the telephone telling Headquarters they'd found the vehicle owned by the suspected kidnapper in the Marazzi case. It was a Lancia Beta Spider. He gave the licence plate details.

Gigi pressed his foot down further on the accelerator and watched with glee as the speedometer went past seventy, then eighty before flickering around the ninety mark. With the wind rushing through his hair, he felt alive.

Nothing was going to stop him from claiming his new life. Not even the police roadblock up ahead.

About the author

Marek Z. Turner is an English writer whose fiction primarily focuses on those for whom life hasn't been kind to.

His work encompasses the crime fiction, noir, and thriller genres, with a dash of black humour thrown in. He has written the novels 'Killerpede', and 'The Eighth Hill', as well as several published crime short stories. He has also written several non-fiction articles on Italian film published across a range of magazines and home entertainment releases.

Permanently fuelled by caffeine, he has a passion for Calcio, Italian food, and cynical European crime fiction. In 2021, he was a finalist in the Capital Crime New Voices Award competition, and in 2024 he was named in the final five shortlist for the Black Spring Press 'Crimebits' competition, as judged by Lee Child.

For the latest publication news, short stories and more, please visit **www.poliziotturner.com**